MAIN STREET, SIBERIA

To Ted & Marianne

continuing Comrades

with Joy!

Dale

11 Dec-2012 A.D.

"Pacific Russia" includes the Russian Far East and most of the area of East Siberia as shown here.

MAIN STREET, SIBERIA

The Surprising Human Capital on the Pacific End of Russia

Dale M. Heckman

VANTAGE PRESS
New York

Permission to reprint map of Pacific Russia (p. ii) granted by *Russia Far East Update,* Seattle, Washington.

Partial support for this research came from AkademLink, Inc.

FIRST EDITION

Published by Vantage Press, Inc.
516 West 34th Street, New York, New York 10001

Manufactured in the United States of America
ISBN: 0-533-12967-2

Library of Congress Catalog Card No.: 98-94062

0 9 8 7 6 5 4 3 2 1

To my parents, Raymond Heckman and Mary Heckman, who were always ready to propose, "let's just go and find out."

Contents

Preface

Through more than four decades of Cold War—1948–1991—Americans and others had only traditional stereotypes with which to think about Siberia and the Russian Far East. Vast uninhabited forest, steppe and tundra, deep cold, land of exiles, slave labor—these vivid images loomed behind nearly all discussion about the east end of Russia. These images still are reflected in questions put by educated audiences to a speaker about current life in those regions—the Pacific end of Russia. Americans have seen photos of muddy log villages with no indoor plumbing and no paved roads, with soot-covered hovels of miners. They have read in detail about vast ecological tragedies including the decline of animal species in trackless wilderness, and of course, the horrible history of gulags in Siberia. Yet Americans generally—even in the 1990s—have not seen the contemporary urban face of Main Street, Siberia.

Suddenly in the Gorbachev era, westerners who ventured to Asian Russia—when they got off the train, beyond gift shops and archives—found large cities with broad paved streets, trams, buses, and soon a growing traffic of private automobiles. One Siberian city of 1.5 million already (even before 1986) had a subway system. A dozen others with populations over 200,000 already enjoyed live opera, ballet, and philharmonic and chamber orchestras in modern concert halls. Yes, and rock concerts. (*Pop quiz: Can you pronounce the name, then point on a map to the city of Ulan Ude? In 1992 its youth, of Buryat and other ethnicity, crowded into a series of Verdi operas, quality productions beginning with "Otello."*)

On the main streets of Siberia as the 1980s ended, women in smart-looking suits, carrying briefcases, clearly were taking pride in their appearance—contrary to western stereotypes. Such new images could no longer be tossed off as the enthusiasm of a first-time tourist. Now anyone could go check it out, and North Americans slowly began doing so. One can still visit the gulag sites, trace the trails of prisoner despair, exhaustion and frostbite, investigate environmental crimes. Yet in the cities, where a very large majority of the population now lives, one finds a different reality.

This is not to claim the old stereotypes were entirely wrong. Siberia and Russia's Far East[1] still cover vast areas of tundra, forest, and steppe, most of it with Canada-type climatic conditions. There are both pristine wilderness and appalling pollution in places where—for North Americans—"our weather begins." Many villagers—even some city dwellers—still carry water from a common well or pipe. Industrial pollution takes many forms. But the first message of this book is that pivotal changes have occurred during recent decades. The population has become predominantly urban. The educational level—attained at regional institutions—has steadily increased. Among the highly educated, most now choose to stay and develop their family network here, several time zones east of the Ural Mountains.[2] This urban society feels surprisingly familiar to a cosmopolitan American visitor.

Point two of this book is that, in the context of current changes in Pacific Russia, a pivotal role belongs to higher education institutions. Modern societies realize that their most precious resource is their highly educated people—more adaptable to changing conditions, capable of deliberate, continuous learning and invention. This book offers first-time information about the region's own sources of highly trained manpower.

For Russia's eastern regions to outgrow their traditional status as colonies for western Russia, they must attain self-sufficiency in preparing highly skilled manpower—homegrown leaders, teachers, researchers, engineers, physicians, and others. So have they?

For these regions to become full partners in the economy of the Pacific Rim, firms and institutions of the U.S., Japan and others must find capable counterparts here, must see that they can collaborate for mutual benefit. So have they?

On their part, leaders of Russia's eastern regions have little patience left for exploitation of their raw resources by outsiders, whether the "outsiders" come from Moscow or from foreign countries. They want primary control of their regions' economic destiny. For this they prefer to attract knowledgeable partners from elsewhere on the Pacific Rim—both academic and commercial. They want to show outsiders that Siberians and Far Easterners can contribute more to a joint enterprise than raw materials and laborers such as loggers, fishermen, and oilfield "roughnecks." Can they?

Universities and other institutions of higher education play a key role in answers to these questions. This book presents new information and firsthand observations that will inform discussion about these regions and their new role in the economy of the Pacific basin. It focuses attention on higher education in eastern Russia—now the main source of the region's highly skilled manpower and womanpower. On that issue, and not on "how to get the resources out," will depend the long-term pacific relations of other nations with these irenic peoples of the Russian Federation.

A note about style.

Since this book's first purpose is to present fresh research information, it is written in the impersonal style of a research report, a style nicknamed "pinstripe passive." Yet most of these findings come from interviews and on-site visits that were unique and, in most cases, warm from the beginning (1986), so I do not want to lose the beating pulse of the encounters. Even from a scientific standpoint, context and first impressions can be important, but the personal adventure of getting around and getting acquainted solo in long-forbidden places, plus the ready welcome extended to me there, simply holds a lot of human interest. Besides, my daughters have asked for the whole story! So a separate, future effort will contain personal narratives and impressions from my 1986 through 1996 *komandirovki* (working journeys) through Eastern Siberia and the Russian Far East.

Risks of Book-writing During Rapid Transition.

Even as finishing touches are being applied to the text of this report, Russia's economic transition skids into a new crisis. This one combines an economic with a political crisis. For several years the funds for paying salaries in higher educational institutions have arrived from Moscow either several months late, or as a reduced percentage of the amount owed, or both. Only yesterday the ruble underwent a new plunge in value. Under such circumstances, university and institute personnel in Pacific Russia will do whatever they need to do for the subsistence of their families—meaning their extended family networks. One cannot foresee how higher educational institutions will fare or even survive in the near term.

Yet exactly because of the present rapid flux and "time of troubles" (a historical reference familiar to Russians!), one can see what a marvelously adaptable organism is a European-type institution of higher learning. Finding themselves caught in the same oceanic turbulence as all their co-workers, academics here do not rush for an attorney to sue for "their contractual rights," they do not tend to pull out the rule book nor report long absences of colleagues from their posts. Not that there's great camaraderie or trust among co-workers; often it is quite the contrary. But in such general conditions of social crisis, the academic person (in Pacific Russia, at least) *tends* to choose a "live-and-let-live" attitude, to accommodate the survival needs of oneself and therefore one's co-workers. People hunker down.

For that reason, the higher educational institutions of Pacific Russia probably will pick up about where they left off, when the present crisis ends. People will return to positions they never left, the rules will be like those which people had tacitly agreed not to enforce, youth will beg for admission to learning mental disciplines they have not yet understood nor agreed to. Most will want, as soon as basic things become stable again, to resume their place in an organized structure that offers expertise for getting things done in rational order in their own region. Thus it makes sense to believe that the research information presented here will retain validity and value, in the mid- and long-term. If that does not prove to be the case, however, then let this report stand to mark a unique historical moment, let it outline a story of how the academic community in Pacific Russia boldly adapted institutions, during a most dynamic decade, for full participation in the academic ferment and the economy of the Pacific Rim.

Notes

1. See Chapter 1, for definition of "Pacific Russia."
2. In fall 1995 the Far East Institute of Economic Research (Motrich) reported a slight decline in population, due both to emigration and to lower birthrate. According to this information, those leaving the region included people from all educational levels but disproportionately from the more educated.

Acknowledgments

During more than ten years of travel, interviewing, and other research in this project, I have received many kinds of help from many kinds of people. I'm afraid I won't name them all here.

For a basic list of higher educational institutions across Siberia, 1984 onward, Alexander Saveliev, Director of the Soviet Research Institute on Higher Education, generously provided copies of the annual Soviet directory. Before I boarded the Trans-Siberian express in 1986, for my first solo journey across Siberia, Anatoli Belyaiev—Moscow editor and journalist—volunteered to telephone colleagues at my stopover cities for help. That October as I visited Khabarovsk State Pedagogical Institute, nonetheless, I walked in unknown; and Prorector Svyetachev still set up a meeting next day for my questions! He later sent the first written curricular details for my project.

Back In California, Valeria Druzhnikov, M.D., invested a lot of hours and creativity in improving my Russian language skills to a level fit for doing my own interviewing.

In fall 1992, my nine-week, seven-city interviewing journey around eastern Russia really became possible when host families agreed to take me into their homes for a week or two in each city: in Khabarovsk, the V. Yakovlevs; in Vladivostok, the L. Prigunovs; in Chita, the M. Maksiutins; in Ulan Ude, the A. Kononovs; in Yakutsk, the V. Nikitins; in Irkutsk, the A. Novikovs; in Birobidjan, the Weiss family. This was a new kind of trip at a tender new moment in U.S.-Russian relations. These folks gave this American stranger much more than a bed, meals, and their doorkey.

The hero who literally travelled ahead of me to arrange for five of those seven hosts is Anatoli Khitrunov, gentle geologist of Khabarovsk. On my later trips, additional hosts included: the V. Balyuk, V. Zadvernyuk, and Y. Kovrigin families (Khabarovsk); and Y & Z Broido (Irkutsk). The Lysov and Pospelova homes (Khabarovsk) were always open to me for supper, local advice, and sociability.

Prof. Susan Hardwick gave a steady current of encouragement and helpful references through the life of the project, including invitations to lecture on its findings. At crucial points, I also received practical encouragement and comment from three University of Hawaii experts—first Librarian Pat Polansky, then Professors John Stephan and Robert Valliant, and an early opportunity from Prof. David Whitaker, U. of British Columbia, to publish an "interim report" of findings. Prof. Anna Scherbakova, Monterey Institute, has given much cheerful support for fashioning new academic linkages with eastern Russia. And Marc Irish, patient computer-tutor and expert, was absolutely the first to pay the compliment of requesting a copy of this book when finished.

Hundreds of academic and business people in Pacific Russia (East Siberia and Russian Far East) submitted to interviews, most of them openly welcomed the occasion and a score of them more than once.

At Irkutsk State University (1986), Rector Yurii Kozlov (after his workday on the road) hosted me for a private two-hour orientation to that institution. Beginning with a presentation about the library's rare book collection, that was a magic moment of collegial welcome. On subsequent visits I enjoyed the genial help also of Prorector V. I. Dmitriev and the library staff.

From 1992 onward, I relied greatly on help from various persons at the Khabarovsk State Polytechnic Institute (*now* Technical University). After two stimulating conversations and dinner with Rector V.K. Bulgakov, I received continuous cooperation from A. Gubenko (Prorector for International Affairs) and unstinting help from the ranking head of that office, Natalya I. Yefremova. Ms. Yefremova has helped in strategic moments as interpreter, and generally as expediter of my work in the Khabarovsk territory, a "comrade" in the best sense of that word. Prorector A.V. Alexandrov, Dean Davydov and Dean Smirnov immediately saw the significance of my inquiry and provided valuable information. The English language faculty took me in as one of their own, and I'm grateful for their friendship.

At the Khabarovsk State Ped. Institute (*now* University), Professors N.R. Maksimova, G. Il'inykh, and Nelli Serkova made it possible for me to join the teaching faculty. At the Irkutsk Institute of Foreign Languages (*now* University), Rector E.P. Tyukavkina welcomed me in 1986 and on my every visit afterward; Professors A. Kuplyanenko and Zh. Aseeva took extra time to gather requested data. So did Prof. Olga Bogomolova and Dean N.V. Yazykova at the Ped. Institute, Ulan Ude. Prof. G-N. Dandaron, first rector of Buryat State University, honored me two successive years with invitations to official gatherings.

At the East Siberian Technological Institute, Prof. L. Mikhedova gave generously of her time, as did V. Tykheev. At the Far East Academy of Railway Transport, T. Silukova provided essential summary data for the territory. At the Khabarovsk Medical Institute, Prorector Suleimanov gave me a useful, just-published federal report which would have escaped my attention. Elsewhere, a librarian will remain anonymous who hinted that a certain administrator had multiple copies of a directory and might give one up if approached in a certain way. Bless all the VUZ librarians!

At Yakutsk University, Prorectors Alekseev and Ishkov, through V. Nikitin, K. Fyodorova, and B. Popov, put me in touch with nearly every dean. At Birobidjan, Rector A. Surnin welcomed me (1992) warmly with a memorable conversation about the beginnings of his institute. In Vladivostok, Prorector R. Misbakhovich and Prof. A. Khamatova quickly arranged interviews with colleagues at Far East State University; Prof. N. Yakobson at the Far East Maritime Academy capped off my interviews there with a water-borne tour of the harbor!

Indeed at almost every institution visited (see list in footnotes to chapter 4), the rector plus selected staff and faculty members readily provided information I requested, often regarding me as more of a colleague than a visiting stranger.

John McDonagh best represents a small cluster of North Americans—businesspersons, foundation representatives, and academic project officers—in the Far East who went out of their way to help. Near the end of my first visit to his office, John McD. asked, "So do you want to use a desk, share our (company) office, use a phone here?" Nancy Luther at the Russian-American Business (training) Center also showed that kind of accommodation. The sense of openness and mission among a couple dozen Americans working in the Russian Far East made me proud. The root system of new relationships across the North Pacific is organic and seems bound to grow, mostly because of such persons on both sides.

MAIN STREET, SIBERIA

1

Inside Eastern Russia Today—An Urban People of the 1990s

The Pacific coastline of the Russian Federation measures more than 7,200 miles, not counting any islands.[1] That is more than six times the length of the California coast. Yet curiously, many highly-educated North Americans miss Russia when thinking about what countries the Pacific Rim includes. When they think of Russia, their mind travels across the Atlantic.

More significantly, what lies behind Russia's Pacific coastline is a diverse population that has steadily become urbanized—by 1989 Siberia and the Far East together were already more than 75 percent urban. These people, moreover, have been furthering their education and training increasingly beyond high school levels. In addition, through TV, cinema, music and now direct personal contacts they have increasingly detailed impressions of American life. Yet from habit of the Cold War decades, Americans and others still tolerate a blank space on their own mental maps of that end of the Russian Federation. So now, "discovering" city after modern city on the east end of the Russian Federation has the effect, for many, of seeing a completely new country emerge out of the mists of the northwest Pacific basin.

What follows in Chapter 1 will orient the reader to the urban life of Pacific Russia, by now about 80 percent of its population. Other chapters introduce the highly educated portion of the population and their institutions of higher education, and show their connection with the emerging economy of this huge region, once nearly forgotten yet bordering on the North Pacific.

"Pacific Russia"—a Definition.

In this book, the term "eastern Russia" or "Pacific Russia" includes those regions of the Russian Federation stretching generally frøm Irkutsk and Lake Baikal eastward across 85 degrees of longitude to the Pacific. (See map, Fig. 1.) Below is a partial list of major cities in Pacific Russia, their 1989 populations, and growth from 1979. Four of these cities stand geographically closer to San Francisco than to Moscow.

Table 1: Twelve Cities of Pacific Russia at Time of Opening to Westerners

City:	Pop. 1989:	10-yr. incr.:
Chita	366,000	21%
Blagoveshchensk	209,000	20
Bratsk	256,000	19
Irkutsk	626,000	14
Khabarovsk	600,000	14
Komsomol'sk na Amure	315,000	19
Nakhodka	160,000	24
Petropavlovsk-Kamchatski	269,000	25
Ulan Ude	353,000	18
Vladivostok	634,000	18
Yakutsk	187,000	23
Yuzhno Sakhalinsk	159,000	12

(Sources: *Chislennost' naseleniya RSFSR po dannym vsesoyuznoi perepisi naseleniya 1989 goda,* Moscow 1990; and *Current Digest of the Soviet Press,* 41/17 (1989). With thanks to Prof. Gary Hausladen, U. Nev. Reno.)

Geographically the eastern slope of Russia begins approximately on the west side of Lake Baikal, includes Yakutia (Republic of Sakha) on the north and extends eastward to the Pacific shoreline. Although the Angara flows northwest from Baikal, urban Russians in Ikutsk tend psychologically to orient themselves toward the Pacific. This should not surprise anyone. From Irkutsk, 17th, 18th, and 19th century hunters, explorers, scientists and missionaries headed toward the North Pacific. The Siberian headquarters of the Russian-American Company was planted in Irkutsk to oversee company operations in Alaska and California. An eastern governor for the tsar had his headquarters in Irkutsk.

In this region, of course, indigenous peoples are Asian, not European. On its southern edge, the border drops eastward from Mongolia to China; this China border, formed mostly by the Amur River (Chin.: Heilongjiang), flows eastward into Pacific waters. On the north, Yakutsk before the railroad was an important point on overland routes to the Pacific. It may become so again, and in 1992 the University of Yakutia (Sakha) pointedly established a new Department of *Pacific* Economic Relations. In recent years, numerous schools and colleges from Irkutsk eastward have added East Asian languages to their curricular offerings.

In sum, increased flexibility and need in the 1990s has enabled people of this vast eastern portion of the Russian Federation to turn more toward their Pacific neighbors for economic and other ties. It can fittingly be nick-named "Pacific Russia" to remind us of that shift.

Multicultural and calm.

The eastern end of the Federation has additional cause to take the name "pacific": it remains in the 1990s a more irenic region than others of the Federation. Historians and elders recall a time early this century when some proposed a truly independent Russian Far East. Again in this decade some regions have declared greater autonomy of one kind or another. Yet an ambitious China to the south sits like a large, grinning cat watching for unwary "strays," and most of these folks are not unwary. But placid? Yes. Informal family conversations frequently point out to a visitor that, here, indigenous peoples like the Buryat and Yakut mingle, work and marry with Russians, Ukranians, Jews and others among them without rancor or suspicion. It is a matter of pride to call oneself a real *"Sibiryak"*—home-grown in Siberia—much like an Alaskan boasting that his parents home-steaded in Alaska. True, many residents here resent any more "outsiders from Moscow" coming "in" to manage or make decisions about regional matters. But they express a placid acceptance of diverse neighbors who have grown up here or settled here permanently. "Here" (hosts often assure one) "it is not like in the western part of the country. We know how to get along with one another." An adjective often used to describe this is *"spokoinoi"*—gentle, calm.

Urban Style.

In 1986, the year after Gorbachev became leader of the USSR, a visi-tor to Khabarovsk could already observe shops along the main street that

3

spruced up their windows and acted like competitive businesses. The retail store of a seafood cooperative adorned its display windows with carved wooden latticework, and covered an exterior wall of the building with ceramic tiles with fanciful designs of sea life. By 1992 a major bookstore and a women's fashion shop also featured colorful, artful displays behind clean plate glass windows. A ground-level *kvass* (light rye beer) bar got into the new spirit with an artfully carved wooden door. The new mercantile awareness seemed always to begin by installing more inviting doors. Even off the main streets shops began trying to become more attractive. By fall 1993, large signboards advertised medical insurance, banks, and other services. Stores advertised that they had lower prices than the competition. The cooperative seafood store on main street remained in business as did the bookstore and the women's fashion shop mentioned earlier.

Similar phenomena could be seen in cities from Vladivostok to Irkutsk. The dull gray "generic" shop appearance—which in 1986 still predominated in Russia—in the east had given way to making retail stores attractive. Single snapshot impressions do not capture what was happening here. In 1992, for example, an observant traveller noted wryly that "all Siberia needs a fresh coat of paint!" Large public buildings especially showed long neglect. But one year later walking the same streets, the traveller grinned, "They're painting *all Siberia!"*

New public buildings, moreover, sprang up to fulfill old promises to regional peoples. A new Buryat Artists Hall, for instance, and a Yakut People's Theater finally appeared with modern, sculpted exteriors stating artistic themes of those republics. An impressive new chamber music hall arose in Birobidjan, capital of the Jewish Autonomous Oblast'.

In personal attire, the "dumpy" look was already on its way out in 1986. By the 1990s along main streets of Siberia women of all ages showed pride in their appearance. One often noticed tram passengers reading western fashion magazines. On September afternoons one might notice an after-work promenade of women, apparently professional and office workers, walking in pairs and clusters, wearing tailored raincoats and dresses, fashionable boots and hats, cosmetics freshly applied. Among the younger set the washed denim look had invaded from Scandinavia and America; a new word "jeansy" (plural) became standard Russian. As in America, overpriced sport shoes began coming from Asian factories. Tee-shirts claim to come from places in America and Europe. (Occasional misspelling betrays other origins). Overall, to an outsider from North Amer-

4

ica, the biggest surprise nowadays consists of how familiar everyone looks here, not how exotic.

Urban Renewal.

By 1995, cities began to complete some major improvements of infrastructure. Khabarovsk citizens endured replacement of miles of water mains; Vladivostok visibly caught up with some major street repairs despite serious energy shortages. Despite horrendous financial stringency, they also paid attention to local cultural treasures. Khabarovsk completed a major renovation of its antique regional library building. Irkutsk did the same for its *oblast'* (county) children's library. Public restoration and preservation of many 19th-century houses got serious during this period. Yet all this does not begin to tell about the opening of innumerable small enterprises nor, for that matter, about the closing of many large factories.

Distribution.

As in Canada, the population of Siberia tends to concentrate close to its southern border between the 50th and 55th parallels. In general, this focuses on the east-west corridor of travel and commerce formed by the Trans-Siberian Railroad. Western Siberia has the largest concentrations, and the population of Novosibirsk (1.5 million) is tied together by a modern subway running under the Ob' River. When the Soviet Union dissolved, many individuals of the indigenous peoples of Siberia—Buryats around Lake Baikal, for instance—began to find their way back home from wherever they had scattered in Soviet places farther west. In general, however, they did not return to their villages, but to cities.

Suburbs and Dachas—the economy-saver.

On the outskirts of cities small stacks of fresh lumber become new or renovated private dwellings. Some of this activity reflects actual population growth, while some of it reflects a "flight to the suburbs." In this case, "the suburbs" means a ring of small dachas (pronounced dotcha, which rhymes with the American "gotcha") and garden lots around each city. Apartment dwellers of the cities thus expand their housing space by building a cabin on one corner of an assigned country garden lot. As many as one in four dacha families adds a *banya* (Russian sauna with steam and stimuli for the skin) in another corner of the garden.

One should not think of the dacha only as a vacation place, a retreat spot afforded mainly to officials and artists. Today in Pacific Russia the dacha functions as the family farm, a small garden plot not far from town where a family can raise a good portion of its own food. A large proportion of apartment dwellers, people of very modest means, now have a dacha. Only this institution allows the economic transition to work or, at least, have its day.

Often the dacha on a garden plot consists of a tiny cottage—two rooms, kitchenette, loft—with outdoor privy. Most of these garden plots, it appears, stand near enough to the cities to be reached by municipal bus connections and, indeed, form a growing suburban ring around the major cities. On Friday through Sunday in summer and fall one sees people crowding the bus stops on their way to and from their dachas and gardens.

In Irkutsk, in October 1993, one could infer the large-scale economic importance of the dacha from a certain act by local governments. Warnings had come by TV about a hard frost on the coming weekend. So, with only a day's notice, both city and regional governments declared Friday/Saturday an official holiday so people could go to their gardens and harvest all they could save from the freezing ground. Old and young put on rubber boots, carried shovels and bags to the bus stop and spent "potato weekend" completing this vital private harvest.

At their dachas in the southern corridor, families raise beets, berries, carrots, cabbage, cucumbers, eggplant, garlic, geese, honeybees, herbs, melons, onions, pears, potatoes, tomatoes, and flowers. (All these have been observed on a single garden plot near Khabarovsk.) Certain berries count as medicinal or therapeutic. But the potato is king.

More than one seasoned housewife may confide that, for her own spirit, the banya at the dacha provides some of her most precious moments, alone and free from immediate demands of others. It promises one delicious hour of private lollygagging.

So the dacha does provide respite from apartment life, pollution and city stress, but in general does not promise physical relaxation. It has become a principal institution for private survival and health in Pacific Russia. It deserves mention as a significant enabler of the transition to a new economic system.

Housing.

Everyone has housing, except for some new refugees beginning to arrive from former Soviet republics far to the west. In the typical 9-story apartment house, most apartments are small by American standards—also very low cost by U.S. comparison. Visitors to California from Siberia often wonder aloud why Americans want so much house space to collect so many possessions. Yet their own furnishings, referring here to the more educated, attest to a decent level of life—color TV, tape deck, sets of hardback books in standard bookcases of polished wood with glass doors. Personal computers and computer games are not uncommon. A teenager's room can look like one in the U.S.; some families even find space for a piano. Kitchens are usually small, yet accommodate the kitchen table where a family eats. For special occasions, the living room converts to a dining room; some major furnishings are designed for dual purpose.

More than one woman has remarked that, if the housing shortage were suddenly eased, many marriages probably would dissolve. Also, more than one couple after divorcing occupies the same apartment for additional years—*he* claims the legal right to some living space, and that there's no other equivalent place for him to move, and *she* continues to prepare meals for him, while maintaining her right to sanctuary. In a variant of the same problem, a married couple intending to stay married (and already with one child) cannot yet live together because neither husband nor wife could tolerate moving into the mother-in-law's apartment. In another variant, a couple declares legal divorce *at first* only to enable him to "move" to another city to claim his deceased mother's apartment there. Visitors now find vacant apartments for rent, and real estate agencies have sprouted up. But "real estate property" still is being defined.

Each year now, new single-family dwellings make their appearance. Most are built of brick, with metallic sheeting on the roof. In a neighborhood of old wooden *"izba"* (cabins) someone builds the sturdy 3-story house of his dreams. Or as part of a cluster of such "cottages" (*kottédj;*) in Russian, even if it's a mansion) on the edge of the city. At first the newly wealthy built not only spacious houses but structures designed to look expensive or powerful—small castles with turrets and towers. Then more modest designs, with contemporary means of temperature control, began to appear. For most professional people, who still hold public-paid jobs and live in cramped apartments, such "cottages" only accentuate the growing income gap in post-Soviet society.

Further Signs of the Market Spirit.

Advertising by private enterprises quickly appeared in the early '90s. Medical insurance, banks, rallies by foreign evangelists, local stores—these head the list. But advertising was not the only accommodation to the new spirit of "the market." In the early 1990s, even in post offices one began to encounter polite clerks! Stores had increasing supplies on the shelf, and seldom did long lines appear. The main consumer problems were now high prices and severe monetary inflation. Bank loan rates became exorbitant (by western standards), based on inflation rates. What interest rate would you charge today if your money will be worth 20 percent less in six months?

In October 1993 a trade fair in downtown Irkutsk featured exhibits not only from foreign companies, such as pharmaceutical firms from France, Germany, and the U.S., but also from many new firms founded in the region itself. The fair filled not only the largest civic indoor sports arena but also other buildings in the city. Visitors paid a substantial admission fee, and weekday attendance appeared good. What could better signal, "We feel ready for business!"

Sibiryaki commonly remark that the new small businesses are mostly traders, most sell foreign import goods to their countrymen. Who now *produces* anything? How can Siberia attract new monies into its economy from outside? Indeed, most local factories—mainstays of the previous system—stand idle. They often express concern that a market requires goods *and/or* services from both/all sides to endure. So, while unaware of many American business conventions and terms, Siberians early showed a grasp of some basic market theory!

Self-reliance.

Siberians in general have a reputation for self-reliance. Many families in the populous southern regions provide much or most of their own food as already described. Frontier experience here as elsewhere has encouraged a "do it yourself" attitude. Enormous individual energy now goes into small business start-ups and, as discussed below, students in large proportions choose to major in business/management/finance specialties. Perhaps it is more telling, however, that the men try to perform their own car repairs and, failing that, search for knowledgeable friends to do the repairs on a barter basis—today's catch, for example, from the river, or an afternoon at the agency's *banya*.

Yet the *interdependence within* an extended network of family and close friends remains a key aspect of "self-reliance"; it is by no means an individualistic matter, a Thoreau-alone-in-the-wild kind of phenomenon. It resembles more the family cooperative of America's earlier times. It is common for an east-Russian university student visiting America to feel keenly unhappy, partly as a result of the absence of supportive older women of his family—a *babushka* (grandmother) or an all-providing *mama*—and partly because fawning Americans expect him to appreciate the superiority of each commercial wonder they expose him to. Meanwhile he is wondering, "With whom can I discuss this for other sympathetic opinions? Is everything American superior? It doesn't feel good to decide all this individually, on my own." This does not negate, however, the general fact that Siberians show greater self-reliance than their countrymen in European Russia. It remains to be seen whether another generation of urbanized youth will deplete this characteristic of self-reliance, relative to western Russians.

The Changes on Main Street.

Strolling up a city's main street and noting some of its recent external changes will help to illuminate the urban nature of life in Pacific Russia, *and* today's strong efforts to update its infrastructure. For such a walk-through, the city of Khabarovsk provides a representative place. This important city has neither the drama of an all-year seaport (and naval hub) as in Vladivostok, nor the historic (300-year) charm of central Irkutsk. Yet its changes represent those occurring in urban centers of Pacific Russia during the decade following 1986.

The city of Khabarovsk (founded 1858; current pop. 600,000) serves as chief entry port to Russia for air travellers crossing the Pacific. It sits on the right bank of the huge Amur River just where the river turns northward from the China border to meander on for five hundred more miles to Pacific waters of the Okhotsk Sea. The city hosts a military complex for guarding the 2,600-mile China border, yet retains the feel of a civilian city. In addition to its air and river traffic, Khabarovsk is on the Trans-Siberian Railroad and a paved highway to Vladivostok. It hosts eight public institutions of higher education. It is as near to San Francisco as it is to Moscow (Kamchatka is *much* nearer). Although hard hit by financial troubles of Russia's federal government, Khabarovsk plays an increasing role in the Pacific Rim economy.

Our walking tour begins at a promontory overlooking the Amur River. Here a city park extends along the high bluff and down to the water's edge. From this park the main street of Khabarovsk runs eastward along a natural ridge, eventually leading to the international airport. Both the north and south sides of this ridge slope gently downhill two blocks to slender valleys that parallel the main street. Along each of these parallel valleys runs a park with trees and split boulevard, and on the far side each one slopes upward again to another major street that also runs eastward from the river. So, historically and now economically, too, Khabarovsk really "begins at the river." Today it stretches for miles along the right bank.

Retouching history.

On the promontory overlooking the river, after the Gorbachev revolution, citizens replaced a Soviet-era statue with a bronze sculpture of Governor-General Muravyev-Amurskii. In the middle of the nineteenth century this Nikolai Muravyev secured Russia's control of the fertile Amur basin and once, sailing past this promontory, declared a city would rise here. The city did arise in 1858 after Muravyev, in the tsar's name, signed the territorial Treaty of Aigun with China. Standing on this spot today we look southwest to low mountains marking the Heksir Wilderness Preserve. Beyond that, perhaps twenty miles from where we stand, lies Manchuria. Freighters and barges busily ply the river now, patrolled by armed cutters. The selection of this pre-Soviet officer-statesman as the one whose statue should now watch over the bend of the Amur makes a strong statement about beginning another era here.

After serving in Pacific Russia for two productive decades, Muravyev was rewarded by the tsar with a rank of nobility and renamed, "Muravyev-Amurskii." Now as we turn away from the river and his statue, we look across a large square, from which the main street begins. The city recently renamed the first mile or so of this street from "Karl Marx" to "Muravyev-Amurskii Street."

New restoration.

As we face the city from this large square, we could walk two blocks to the left where the Khabarovsk Region has newly renovated its museum of natural history and now works on the historical museum next door. Across the street from it stands the old Far East military museum, which now also houses a commercial shop selling fine jewelry of amber. Closer to us on the left is the office of a joint venture (Russian/U.S.) in electronic communication systems. Or we could walk to the right one hundred yards, where a joint Russian/Japanese venture has renovated and enlarged a historic "mansion with a view." The building now houses an exclusive small hotel and offices for several firms, principally Japanese. Down that street stand a few other new or handsomely renovated buildings serving (predominantly) Japanese businessmen, including a ground floor walk-down labelled "Fitness Klub."

While we talk on the edge of this square, trolley-buses as well as diesel buses turn around here in rapid succession, and begin their various routes up Muravyev-Amurskii. Though most people depend on public transport, there also is heavy automobile traffic. So, very carefully crossing the square, we pass a party of Korean-Russians taking wedding-day photos at a monument. Beyond them, on the east edge of the square, stands a striking old building of gray stone, red brick, and fanciful nineteenth-century architecture. In 1995–96, this, the regional library, finally shed the scaffolding of an extensive renovation and again serves as a showpiece of civic architecture. Its staff meanwhile built active ties with colleagues in Pacific America, attending meetings of the American Slavic Studies Association and library conferences.

Public regard for style.

Next-door to the library once stood another old, but in this case decrepit, building until some enterprising Japanese came to town. According to a local resident, the Japanese proposed to build in its place a large modern restaurant with hotel accommodations attached on the side away from the street. But local people feared losing the street's architectural integrity—the grand effect stated by the library building and others facing it from across the street. So the Japanese came up with a design and materials (mainly brick) that do not clash, and now have perhaps the most prominent—and expensive—restaurant in downtown Khabarovsk. Nearby, the same firm wisely maintains a modest groundfloor cafe, more intimate and within price reach of more of the local Russians.

One of the low, classic brick buildings across the street from the restaurant is the drama theater for children and youth. Local citizens feel a special affection for this traditional institution, and pride that it still thrives through the present transition. Moving along, we come to some new scaffolding and recognize the former site of the seafood cooperative retail shop, mentioned above. Its fanciful tile panels are gone, and signs announce that it will become a retail outlet for Russian vodka—that is, specifically not for imported stuff.

So, only two blocks into our stroll along "main street," we already see an extensive range of renovation and renewal. It includes significant new enterprises by private investors, but it also features restoration of important public treasures. Were we to turn left here for two blocks, we would see a newly-finished public stairway, as wide as the street which it blocks. Notably, all the steps are of even height, which often did not happen during Soviet times. This handsome granite walkway connects pedestrians to the valley parkway and the sports complex near the river. No parking lots at that complex!

Continuing to the next block on Muravyev-Amurskii Street, we pass a refurbished bakery shop with a constant stock of baked goods and sweets. Long bread lines are a thing of the past here. A couple of buildings past it, plate-glass display windows reveal an elegant jewelry store. Just beyond that, a smaller shop window shows dozens of cameras for sale, most of them with Japanese labels. Such "outward" displays were not part of the Soviet style; this is marketing! Across the street, occupying nearly the whole block, a four-story public building stands newly covered by scaffolding, undergoing sandblasting and painting.

On the next street to the left, illuminated signs tell of two new restaurants. But staying on Main Street, we pass numerous other shops plus sidewalk vendors. These vendors—tending their nylon and pipe-frame stands

Statue of Count Nikolai Muravyev-Amurskii at Khabarovsk park promontory, facing China across the Amur River, 1996.

"Fitness Klub" walk-down, Khabarovsk, 1996.

Antique charm of the "Theatre for Youngsters, Khabarovsk, 1996."

Renovated library on the main street of Khabarovsk, flanked by Sapporo Restaurant, 1996.

through winter and summer—feature especially audiocassettes, fresh fruit and vegetables, clothing and ice cream. A gray stone building with colored glass window designs, recently refurbished inside, houses a *"gastronom,"* a major food market. Upstairs it has a new, bright-colored soda shop for tired shoppers and their kids.

For the whole length of this street, sidewalk is separated from actual street by a wide grassy strip with trees, and a low, cast-iron fence, so nearly all pedestrians use the crosswalks. A refurbished building across the street—early 1900s with turret—catches our eye. This "workers' council" headquarters now also houses a private bank.

Ahead, the roof-line of a three-story, newly painted building attracts our attention. It provides one of the rare reminders that we are in Asia—the same reminders as the roof designs on the railroad terminal buildings at each end of the Trans-Siberian Railroad. The peaks are high and very steep, with small corner towers that provide an air intake under their separate roofs. All the roof surface is a shade of green that suggests copper sheathing. The corner eaves do not turn up pagoda-style, and it is hard to

16

account precisely for the Asian air about it. During Soviet times this interesting building housed the regional headquarters of Young Pioneers, and before that, some provincial government offices. Today its street level shops include a children's book store, a Xerox copy shop, Kodak film-developing center, floral shop, and art store. Painters have just completed repainting the exterior. Local pedestrians pause to admire some careful new design work against ivory and buff-colored walls. They appear satisfied that the paint job does justice to this civic showpiece.

In a neighboring building, a non-profit organization operates art instructional programs for children. Such out-of-school programs definitely have not died out with the demise of the Young Pioneers and Youth Komsomol, former organs of the Party. Around town one finds, for example, several excellent youth ensembles that perform ethnic dances; at least two of these regularly perform abroad. And there are other private schools for children's art. Still, in the hearts of local adults this charming building with the Asian roof-line and neat paint job will remain *"Dom pionerov"* (Young Pioneers Building).

During one recent fall/winter a sidewalk sign announced that a Presbyterian church met on these premises every Sunday, but that congregation now meets in one of the northern districts of the city. Khabarovsk city stretches miles to the north and south of the central district where we now walk.

Diagonally across the intersection stands the central post office, and beneath it an office for long distance telephoning and for paying one's phone bill. Nothing on the outside physically recommends this place except that large signs advertise the various services offered—as though they expect competition. Inside one finds a score of different service windows, standing desks for patrons to complete the addressing of their envelopes, and a card-and-bookshop. In winter one can buy Christmas greetings here, and calendars with Russian religious themes. Yet that is not the biggest news at the post office. From about 1993, Russian-speaking foreign visitors began to report receiving polite, efficient service here. And it is so.

The cross street here still shows signs of an excavation, a narrow ditch that stretched for two blocks or more in both directions from Muravyev-Amurskii Street. That reminds us that this city has replaced mile after mile (kilometer after kilometer) of its water supply and sewage lines—a project occupying most of the past five years.

Time does not permit pausing for comment at every building on main street. New doors with windows in them, display windows without shut-

17

The historic "Young Pioneers Home," artfully refurbished with street-level shops, Khabarovsk, 1996.

Office high-rises along the main street, Khabarovsk, 1996.

Turreted original movie house, amid newer commercial buildings, Khabarovsk, 1996.

Historic restoration behind office high-rise, Khabarovsk, 1996.

New entrance of carved oak at government agency in historic restoration, off Main Street, Khabarovsk, 1996.

ters or iron grids, and advertisements appear everywhere along this colorful route. The gold-leaf sign in front of a securities investment firm causes us to look again and read carefully. Yes, that's what it is. In general, the largest sign boards along this thoroughfare advertise banks and insurance.

An American's access to local government.

Passing the territorial government administrative building, we recall an American's story that, simply by mentioning the name of the official with whom he had an appointment, he received permission from the entrance security officer to find the office upstairs by himself. Not finding his official "in" just yet, this visitor settled down to wait in a large stuffed chair off the corridor. There he dozed off until awakened by hallway conversations as the *duma* (legislature) adjourned and its members passed by him on their way to lunch. So much for Cold War mutual fears!

Cheap flicks from the U.S.

At once we come to *Gigant* (Giant), a 3-screen cinema. According to its weekly posters, at least one of its three films always is American-made, sometimes two. These, however, are not always films that make an American visitor proud. Russian national TV regularly schedules American classic films, and (fortunately) far more Sibiryaki view those than the cinema.

Live drama and mime.

Across the intersection the main drama theatre is closed just now for renovations, but signs announce that it plans to open later this winter. It seems noteworthy that, even during its present budgetary distress, the city government supported renovation of a small theater several blocks from here for a mime troupe. Now in its second year of resurrection, the mime theater *Triad* enjoys vigorous patronage from both local and foreign supporters. It has tackled mime presentations of such classics as Pushkin's "Queen of Spades" and Hemingway's "Old Man and the Sea," in addition to clown shows for children.

About a mile farther east, beyond our stroll of the day, the Khabarovsk Theater of Musical Comedy boasts a modern style building much larger than the mime theater and a program of traveling and local productions, also substantial audiences. The city also supports a symphony orchestra, art museum and various other cultural institutions. An American might get the impression that these people aim local economic efforts toward supporting public cultural interests, rather than the other way around! Although many academic professionals cannot now afford to attend a play or concert for lack of a pay check during several consecutive months, they would generally support that idea.

Huddling next to the drama theater stands a corner cafe, "Snow Princess." Venturing in, we find here plenty of private tables, cafeteria-type counter, and decent restrooms. The counter offers hot dogs, sandwiches, tortes, coffee, tea, hot chocolate and other light beverages—this is not a full meal place. Yet a well-lit walk-in place to sit, unhurried, still seems a luxury. Within a couple blocks on Muravyev-Amurskii stands another such place—an intimate tea room. Waitresses there seem less accustomed to strangers and it is more expensive. It does occur to us that American westerners might prefer the former ("Snow Princess") while easterners or British might prefer the latter style of snack shop.

Department stores.

The main department store (*univermag*) shows no shortage of standard goods, plus a choice of goods from diverse sources. American paper towels, toilet paper, and paper handkerchieves and napkins have made this a necessary shopping stop for the growing English-speaking foreign community in town. The *univermag* also includes a ticket outlet for productions at the musical comedy theater. Last season, the biggest hit was a production of *My Fair Lady*—in Russian language. Some of the merchandise departments here are so separate that the shopper must go outside and down another flight of stairs or around the (outside) corner to get there.

Begging in public.

It is not unusual, nowadays, to find a child sitting alone outside a larger store, on a blanket on the sidewalk with a cup before him for donations. His dark skin and other features tell that he belongs to a family of refugees from a Central Asian Republic, or from the Caucasus. Or an elderly woman, a Russian pensioner, might stand all day holding some small thing to offer in exchange for a contribution. But most of these older ones cluster at the central market and at the main Orthodox church.

Youth hang-outs.

Across the main drag at this point stands the *diskotek,* unpretentious but popular magnet for youth. There is music and there is dancing, but some youth themselves suggest that the essential function is meeting friends, hanging out. (There is, as yet, no indoor mall.) Other locations around the city offer regular events geared for youth—the technical university on the north side, for one. But this one in the central city seems the most popular.

Granite masonry.

Soon we come to the cross street with the trolley line—the light-rail route connecting the southern district of the city with the central district and the railroad station. This street has been divided for many years by the trolley rails and a deep unpaved space between them. Woe to the auto that caught a wheel in that well! But now city work crews have filled the space with crushed rock and are converting the street into a single driving surface with rails down the middle. The pavers have worked in both directions from the Muravyev-Amurskii Street crossing. As this renewal began, some of the old street curbing was destroyed. So the city has installed new curbstone fashioned of granite, rather than more shortlived concrete. Somewhere there still are real stonemasons! Down this cross street for two blocks, both north and south, new trees also have been planted behind the curbing.

Local friends hasten to explain these street improvements. "The mayor soon will stand for reelection, that's why he's making improvements." We explain in response, "So, whatever may be the leaders' motives, democracy (the 'need' to get re-elected) is having its effects." Visible to the north stands a historic preservation project. Here a century-old house rises from red brick walls on its ground floor to vertical wood siding on its second—and top—floor. In its restored form, the vertical siding has been oiled to show off its natural grain. It has two non-profit organizations as tenants.

Re-doing public administration.

In the next block, overlooking large Lenin Square, stands an impressive, five-story gray building, mostly of concrete. Americans might suppose it began life as a bank building. Actually it was the major institution in this region for training managers and officials for the Party structures during Soviet times. The building's interior underwent substantial renovation beginning approximately 1993; the institution itself underwent a couple of new starts and staff changes. Then in 1995 the Office of the (federal) President turned it into the Far Eastern Academy of State Service (public administration), a higher educational institution. In addition to preparation for government service, this Academy also offers majors in business administration and management, and has built strength in computer sciences training for these fields. Its new international office has established relationships with institutions and colleagues in several Pacific Rim countries including the U.S.

Half of this Academy's students are preparing for jobs in the private sector. Actually most institutions of higher education—no matter what their special fields—have added single courses and entire programs in economics, business management and administration. In one, a "Russian-American Center for Business Training" provides short courses in applied business management for local Russian entrepreneurs. But that is at a different academy than this one.

This Far Eastern Academy has student housing on the premises, and in addition it has two or three entrepreneurial ventures. On one end of its block-long structure is a small hotel with a hotel grille. The sign over the door bears the English word, "Hotel," clearly indicating its welcome to English-speaking visitors. At the other end, the ground floor corner space is leased for retailing selected imports. In fact, most institutions of higher education in Pacific Russia work hard to devise ways to use their facilities for income. It is a matter of survival.

On the plaza.

The Academy looks out upon Lenin Square, a spacious pedestrian plaza across which "the white house"—a tall government building covered with white marble—faces the somber brick walls of the medical and pharmaceutical schools. Here in midwinter the city celebrates the New Year, the snow and ice, and "Father Frost," by erecting various ice slides, sleigh rides, and other winter fun for children, parents and youth. On the far side of the plaza a dark statue of V.I. Lenin gestures somberly to all the fun-makers, including those who aim to do a little private business with the winter crowd. The plaza has festive lighting all midwinter. In summer its wide border strips are planted in chrysanthemums.

Can the marketplace be left of Lenin Square?

Here the street of Muravyev-Amurskii jogs left, then right, to go around the plaza, and from here its name reverts to Karl Marx Street. Past the medical institute on the corner stands a major academic bookstore. Three blocks to the left, past a renovated youth center and down a street re-paved and lined with young trees, the central market bustles seven days a week—a large indoor food market ringed round by a larger outdoor bazaar.

Time constraints bring an end to our stroll. For five or six more blocks on Karl Marx Street we would pass other significant public places—some in process of renewal—and private enterprises—some with attractive advertising. Continuing eastward by bus for a few miles, we arrive at the Khabarovsk International Airport. There a new terminal building for international flights was completed in 1995, with amenities similar to those at airports in U.S. cities of comparable size, though not yet as commercialized. The terminal has been designed and built through collaboration between local government and a foreign firm. Clean, well-lighted, it has streamlined its check-in, arrival, and customs procedures compared to what it replaced. It collects a special tax from foreign passengers to help pay for the new terminal.

This stroll-with-commentary along the main street of one city of Pacific Russia touches a fair sample of urban renewal and change. It was not intended to discuss the major industrial (production) plants active or inactive; they're located outside the central district, and their current problems along with the country's economic crises belong to a different discussion than the present one. What our walk-through does richly demonstrate is that local/regional governments have been working diligently in the 1990s to restore and preserve the public's cultural treasures while renovating basic infrastructure.

Summary

Sampling urban sites along and near "main street" conveys the flavor of the current life context of a majority of people in Pacific Russia. Of course, a visitor with a camera would have little problem finding neighborhoods of old-style log houses with unpaved streets, even within city limits. Older Americans remember how Izvestia or Tass journalists selectively described and photographed economically disadvantaged conditions in Harlem or Appalachia in the U.S. Some of those were accurate in detail while untrue as a portrayal of "typical" American life after 1945. Likewise, to describe life today in Pacific Russia without a close-up look at its major cities produces a similar distortion.

The present reality is that urban dwellers of Pacific Russia—80 percent of the 1990s population—walk or drive daily on paved streets and sidewalks. They shop in stores where the main problems have to do not with supply (availability) of goods but with price (affordability), stores with an increasing awareness of competition. The population elects local and territorial governments that realize they must show some product in order to get re-elected. Cities have been paving streets and renovating buildings, generally sprucing up. Their public transportation, despite hurting for repairs and spare parts, remains ahead of most U.S. cities in terms of moving people across town and to suburbs. Some cities, especially Vladivostok, have outrun their energy supply despite abundant potential sources in the region. Other municipal problems gnaw and persist. Unpaid wages of many high-skill citizens press them into serious poverty. Many young graduates must look elsewhere for career jobs. Yet, when viewed over fifteen years, urban living in Pacific Russia has become steadily more attractive.

People here express a strong sense of rootedness; although the grandparents may have migrated here, the middle generation now has an extended family network in place. Even very tough times stir little desire or expectation of moving from the region. Some recruitment by other countries begins to attract the young, highly-skilled to emigrate; but the population thus far remains basically stable.

As symbolized by the new statue of Muravyev-Amurskii, this urban population is acutely aware of its location on the Pacific Rim and the need to develop its own economic relations and strong ties with Pacific neighbors. Whatever may be their problems here, these people show little reluctance to create or engage in private enterprise. And for this they constantly look for suppliers, collaborators, partners from certain Pacific countries including the U.S.

Our stroll found that new sectors of commercial activity have taken root: advertising, travel agencies, insurance, private banking, private publishing. Most people here have never dealt before with a bank, never had a savings account, never paid bills by check, never before 1991 saw a personal credit card. Yet they do not wish to be anyone's colony, ever again, and intend to mature economically. In conversation, academic people express deep frustration over the idle factories or other local production centers. Why does no group of managers, no experienced leader gather the workers to again produce things locally? Some managers from the former system did gather capital and take over production plants, only to sell off and export the equipment! So the hopes must rest on a new generation of initiators and leaders.

Where will such "new generation of initiators and leaders" come from? The Academy on Lenin Plaza, and beyond it the Medical University and the Pedagogical University, all remind us of the surprising array of higher educational institutions in Pacific Russia. From these, and not from somewhere outside, will come that new generation.

Notes

1. This figure, in nautical miles, does not include islands. Information provided by telephone, U.S. Navy Mapping Office.

2

Higher Education in Pacific Russia— A Changing Profile

Along with other industrial countries, Russia officially regards higher education as essential to its well-being, both for economic and for sociopolitical reasons. Its institutions are the vital source of highly educated "human resources." As Chapter 1 put it, from them must come the "new generation of initiators and leaders." So, in the late 1980s, the central government launched a number of changes favorable to higher education even in the eastern regions. By 1992 a steady stream of change marked higher education in Pacific Russia. Then, mid-1990s, the central government reneged on financial support, allowing its investment in higher education there to sink to ruinous levels. Yet even this, ironically, promoted positive changes!

Despite financial neglect from "the center," even those higher educational institutions farthest east of Moscow survive! Despite delays of several months in receiving salaries and stipends, instructors continue to meet classes on schedule, students compete for admission, and prorectors still plan future improvements. This survival under great financial stress must not be glossed over. These institutions are adapting to new conditions, creating new academic forms and even increasing in number. They are a marvel of adapting to survive. And they are preparing the region's own experts for Russia's full participation in the Pacific Rim economy.

During Cold War years, Americans had contact with only a few higher education institutions in Russia and these were in Moscow or Leningrad. In rare instances a western mathematician or physicist might attend a conference as far east as Novosibirsk (West Siberia). Canadian naturalist Farley Mowat and U.S. historian John Stephan are striking exceptions who studied the Far East firsthand pre-*glasnost.* Such limited acquaintance by the west probably resulted both (a) from a Soviet policy to put only their most prestigious academic foot forward and (b) from the number of places deemed "safe" to allow foreigners.[1] Most travel restrictions evaporated along with Party and Soviet structures.

Already in fall 1986, some rectors in Pacific Russia expressed personal interest in developing relations with North American counterparts. In 1991–92, all cities there became "open" to foreigners. Yet even by the mid-1990s, few American institutions had ventured new relationships with universities in regions of Russia oriented toward the Pacific Rim. Lewis and Clark College was one pioneer, in a two-way student exchange with Khabarovsk Teachers College (Pedagogical Institute). The University of Hawaii formed valuable channels for information sharing. Universities of Alaska, Washington, Maryland and Portland State (Ore.) reached out, also the California Maritime Academy. But other prestigious U.S. universities did not leap to this historic opening on the Pacific end of Russia. After September 1992 when the U.S. opened a consulate in Vladivostok, commercial activity by North American firms increased in the region. Still, no organized information about the region's key resource—sources of educated manpower—was available.

So this chapter must first provide a sense of the *scope* of higher education in Pacific Russia—how many institutions of higher education, in what locations, of what nature, of what scale in the population, what special fields? (Appendix A lists the institutions.) The chapter then reports on new institutions founded in this region since 1986–87, and on some already established ones that were upgraded. It then identifies four key policy changes that led to recent substantive changes in the institutions. Finally it discusses some of these changes, including life as an undergraduate.

VUZ: a handy word for "higher educational institution."

The standard term in Russian for higher educational institution is *vysshee uchebnoie zavedenie,* whose first letters form the acronym, *VUZ.* Russians have long used this acronym as a noun, with its plural "VUZy," and that handy practice will be followed here. (Appendix B contains a short list of other terms in education at the postsecondary level, in Russian and American current usage.) Literally the VUZ words mean "higher *instructional* institution," pointing to the important distinction between *institutes for teaching* and *institutes for research (N.I.I.).* Research institutes,

29

operating under the Russian Academy of Sciences, long have been separate from universities and other VUZy. Under the Russian Academy with its Siberian and Far Eastern Branches, research institutes are distributed among major cities of Pacific Russia. Research institutes commonly supervise graduate students, and their researchers often hold joint appointments for lecturing in VUZy.

Scope of Higher Education in Pacific Russia

In 1987, Eastern Siberia had 28 institutions of higher education (VUZy) including two universities; the Far East held 30 VUZy including two universities. (*See Table 2.*) Of the total 58, the most numerous by type were the 14 teacher's colleges (pedagogical institutes), and there were seven polytechnic institutes. The polytechnics enrolled the largest numbers of students. The Irkutsk polytech. in 1992 boasted the "largest enrollment east of the Urals"—9,000 full-time (day) and 15,000 total, while Khabarovsk Polytech had over 11,000 total, and the East Siberian Institute of Technology (Ulan Ude) enrolled 10,000 including 7,000 full-time/day. These technological institutes concentrated on multiple branches of engineering, architecture and other applied technical fields. Early in the 1990s their enrollments plunged, partly by design. This will be discussed further, but as a group they remain the largest VUZy.

Table 2: Higher Education Institutions in Siberia/Far East, 1987
(By Type and Economic Planning Area)

	"Pacific Russia"		
	Western Siberia	Eastern Siberia	Russian Far East
Universities	8	2	2
Polytechnical institutes	5	4	3
Pedagogical institutes	16	6	8
Medical institutes	8	3	3
Agricultural institutes	5	3	3
All other VUZy	35	10	11
TOTALS	77	28	30

(Principal source: *Spravochnik dlya postupayushchikh v VUZy, 1987,* Moscow, annual Soviet "Handbook for those entering higher education institutions, 1987")

Russian universities traditionally have not included the wide array of professional schools and major research units often found in an American university. Schools of medicine and law, for example, have remained separate. Research institutes also remain separate. So Russian universities seem small by American standards. They offer a traditional[2] range of academic disciplines, emphasize theory and prepare students especially for academic professions. The universities are to replenish the ranks of the professoriate. One exception to the pattern is Yakutsk State University. It serves a vast area with sparse population, Yakutia (Sakha) Republic. Here the faculties of medicine and pedagogy (teacher prep) are folded into the single university. The prevailing pattern, however, keeps Russian universities less complex in their structure than public universities in the U.S.

No Pre-Professional tradition.

In the same tradition, separate VUZy, each one specializing in one applied field (except for *poly*technical institutes=diverse engineering), cover a range of subjects not found in university curricula. Separate medical and pedagogical institutes, for example, theater arts and other cultural institutes, institutes for engineering in rail transport and in water transport—as the 1990's began, each of these VUZy prepared students directly after high school for specialized professional work. They have no tradition of *pre*-professional programs (pre-med, pre-law, etc.) or of "breadth" (liberal arts) courses after high school. Each type of VUZ, moreover, "received" its curricular outlines, size of entering class, and finances via the federal ministry pertaining to its special field—ministry of transport, ministry of public health, and so on. In the early 1990s, changes in that system appeared swiftly.

Trade schools.

A separate system of specialized secondary schools/colleges (*uchilishche* and *tekhnikums*) offers programs providing high school completion and two to four years beyond it. These are analogous to American trade/occupational schools and the vocational side of community colleges. While important to the economy of a region, they are not counted part of higher education. The same can be said of various forms of adult education.

New and Renewed VUZy in Pacific Russia.

After 1987, a few new public VUZy emerged in Pacific Russia. The Republic of Buryatia celebrated the opening (fall 1992) of its own university, with Buryat leadership. At its first anniversary party, an outpouring of gifts from all sectors of the community (and China) demonstrated its deep local significance. In 1991 the Jewish Autonomous Oblast' received a teachers' college in Birobidjan, its first VUZ of any type. In 1994 in Khabarovsk a former school of management for the Party bureaucracy, after two incarnations, became a federal academy of public administration for the Far East, with full rank of VUZ. Also, the first private VUZy appeared, taught mainly by instructors moonlighting from the public ones.

Upgrades.

Meanwhile, some VUZy also took steps toward a higher status. The Far East State Maritime Academy (Vladivostok), for example, was upgraded to full VUZ status. Several institutes received university status. Although local faculty members tend to grin wryly about "name-only" changes, such re-naming in at least some cases was preceded by significant changes in the institution. Buryat Ped. Institute actually merged with fledgling Buryat State University. Khabarovsk State Polytechnical Institute created a faculty of liberal arts, added a research center in computer sciences, and increased its international programs. It made other major shifts of staff and emphasis among faculties (schools). Meanwhile it greatly increased the number of graduate students in several faculties including the new faculty of liberal arts (*gumanitarniy*). In 1993 this VUZ became Khabarovsk State Technical University.

The Khabarovsk Institute of Railway Engineering expanded its offerings, especially into electronic communications and market economics and management, increased its international contacts, and became the Far Eastern State Academy of Transport (literally, "of Ways of Communication"—*putei soobshcheniya*). Teachers' college (pedagogical institutes) in Irkutsk, Khabarovsk, Ulan Ude and elsewhere gained university status.

These illustrate status changes of entire institutions. New *programs,* e.g. in market economics, business management and administration, and other curricular additions will be discussed separately.

So a preliminary scanning of Pacific Russia reveals that VUZy in Pacific Russia not only survived the first years of *perestroika* but even increased in number. This by itself constitutes an amazing accomplishment. Secondly, as will be seen, some moved quickly even in the late 1980s but most in the early 1990s to adapt to new economic conditions and regional needs. In the second half of the decade, under dreadful financial conditions, they continue to change.

Distribution.

VUZy in Pacific Russia, as elsewhere in the world, cluster in certain population centers—eight in Irkutsk, for example, eight in Vladivostok, eight in Khabarovsk (1987). These numbers do not include branches (*filialy*) of VUZy with main headquarters elsewhere, nor military engineering colleges nor new private ones. In Irkutsk in 1986, more than one of every ten persons was a student in higher education, and this lent a definite "college town" atmosphere to the central sector of the city. On the other hand, many smaller cities have but one or two VUZy plus branches of other VUZy with headquarters elsewhere. Magadan has a pedagogical institute plus branches of two other VUZy. Chita has three institutes (VUZy) plus four branches. In proportion to the population, VUZy are about as numerous in eastern as in western Russia.

When branches and regular extended learning classes are taken into account, nearly all cities and towns of Pacific Russia have some kind of formal higher education program. In addition, wide and serious use has long been made of extended learning modes in regular undergraduate programs. In the mid-1990s, however, some VUZy began to cut back their extended learning programs for financial reasons. One began to hear of senior faculty members who refused to travel to teaching sites beyond their city if it did not improve their pay considerably. And more than one VUZ, even at its home site, closed its evening division to cut costs of heating, lighting and maintenance.

Higher Learning in Population-at-large.

How do these VUZy—having increased by now to seventy-some in Pacific Russia—appear statistically in terms of the general population? Figures for only the Far East show that in 1994, of every 10,000 residents, 147 were then students in a higher education institution. (When comparing with regional U.S. figures, it is important *not* to count community college enrollments as "higher" education.) In the district of Khabarovsk, however, 237 (of 10,000 pop.) were students in a VUZ. In Vladivostok's Maritime district, it was 175. In fact, on this measure, Khabarovsk ranked seventh among all such census units of Russian Federation. (*See Table 3.*) An official estimate puts the headcount number of students in Khabarovsk district at 38,600 for the year 1992–93.[3] In the Russian Far East, Vladivostok and Khabarovsk are the two main population centers.

Table 3. Fall Enrollments in Higher Education Institutions
(per 10,000 population)

	1985	1990	1994
Russian Federation	206	190	172
Russian Far East	171	152	147
Maritime (Vladivostok) Territ.	238	204	175
Repub. Of Sakha (Yakutia)	83	72	94
Jewish Auton. oblast	—	18	67
Khabarovsk Territory	313	267	237
Amur oblast'	141	133	137
Kamchatka oblast'	43	70	85
Magadan oblast'	74	75	97
Sakhalin oblast'	41	42	47

(From: Sotsial'noe razvitie primorskogo kraia, v sravnenii s sosednimi regionami Irossiei; Vladivostok, 1995. Social development of Maritime Territory compared with neighboring regions and with all Russia.)

A sudden decline in VUZy enrollments in approximately 1989–90, evident in Table 3, is commonly ascribed to (a) a rush by young people into some form of new enterprise, and (b) deliberate cuts in the number of stipend-supported students in some fields and majors. By plan, teaching staffs remained stable, enriching the student/instructor ratio.

In terms of students graduating (Table 4), in 1994 Khabarovsk territory (*krai*) had 38 new graduates per 10,000 residents and Maritime Territory had 30. In the city of Khabarovsk this could translate arithmetically into 2,500 new graduates in 1994, but the city's total is much higher because urban centers have higher proportions of students. (*See Chap. 4.*) On this measure, Khabarovsk territory ranked fifth among all census districts in the Russian Federation.

Table 4: Annual Number of Graduates from Higher Education Institution[4]

(per 10,000 population)			
	1985	**1990**	**1994**
Russian Federation	33	27	28
Russian Far East	26	19	23
Maritime (Vladivostok) Territory	35	25	30
Repub. Of Sakha (Yakutia)	13	11	11
Jewish Auton. oblast'			5
Khabarovsk Territory	48	33	38
Amur oblast'	22	16	20
Kamchatka oblast'	8	8	11
Magadan oblast'	11	11	14
Sakhalin oblast'	6	6	6

From: Sotsial'noe razvitie primorskogo kraia, v sravnenii s sosednimi regionami irossiei; Vladivostok, 1995. Social Development of the Maritime Territory, compared to neighbor regions)

Non-state, Independent Institutions.

New independent (non-state) VUZy quickly began to appear in this period. In Khabarovsk alone, three opened by 1995. Regional branches of other independents doubled this number—for example, a branch of Moscow University of Consumer Cooperatives. In Irkutsk, the Russo-Asian Liberal Arts University opened its doors in 1993 with more than 100 paying students enrolled, an affiliate of a new institution in Ekaterinburg. In order to operate, such institutions must be inspected and licensed by a federal agency. Until experience accumulates, however, it is difficult to categorize them in the spectrum of Russian higher education. (*See Appendix A*)

In Khabarovsk, 1994–5, the President of the Russian Federation established the Far Eastern Academy of Government Service (i.e. public administration). For a brief period it had been the "Personnel Training Center." This Academy also offers business management for the private

35

sector. While not independent, this operates under unique auspices new to the post-Soviet period.

Another new VUZ—an independent one—has the same address as the public VUZ that spawned it! Commonly a group of instructors rent facilities in the VUZ of their primary employment and offer a special program (incl. tutoring, perhaps evening) to students who enroll and pay separately. Joint business degree programs taught by both local and foreign instructors are officially under public universities, but function with great autonomy. Such are the BA program at Irkutsk State University/University of Maryland, at Far Eastern State University (Vladivostok)/ University of Maryland, and at Yakutsk University/University of Alaska.

Current Enrollments.

The size of student enrollments at these VUZy by 1995–96 ranged from under one thousand up to nine thousand. At the turn of the decade, two events happened almost simultaneously to cause an abrupt drop in enrollments. (a) Many young people decided to plunge into some kind of money-making enterprise rather than "lose the moment" by attending college. And (b) many VUZy, through the office of the rector, gained new authority in setting standards and quotas for admitting new students. They no longer, for instance, had to accept over-inflated quotas of "specialists needed" by various industrial enterprises, if those enterprises did not enter into contracts to support the same number of student positions in that VUZ, and provide that number of jobs after graduation.

Although students themselves abruptly shifted their preferences from some fields to others, total enrollments began to stabilize or increase. From 1993 to 1995, overall enrollment at Khabarovsk State Tech. University only crept from 5,340 to 5,361, but at the Irkutsk Institute for Teachers of Foreign Languages from 1,872 to 1,954. At Far East State Academy of Transport the entering class for those years jumped from 1,578 to 2,107. These (latter) figures reflect major changes or additions to the programs previously offered.

Socio-Political Context.

In order to appreciate such "bumpy" changes in VUZy, observers must hold in mind the social context of these years in Pacific Russia. Inflation had already devastated the value of a ruble and continued at a gallop; the salaries of many professionals never caught up with inflation, a new flood of foreign visitors included all kinds—the well-meaning, the opportunists, thieves. Organized crime became privatized. Meanwhile the military draft of young males continued, as did a costly, unpopular war in Chechnya. In the face of such conditions and uncertainties, students and VUZy collectively behaved in rational ways that envisioned some kind of orderly future where higher education would pay off.

Campus Complex Model.

In recent decades the model of Novosibirsk has spread. There in western Siberia in the 1950s, the Soviets formed *Akademgorodok* (Academic Town). Near the eastern shore of a huge reservoir called the "Ob' Sea" and a hydroelectric station, they located a dozen important research institutes (including atomic) and a university in close proximity to one another—in other words, a campus. Apartment houses and dormitories, stores and cinemas plus other recreational facilities surrounded by pine forest make Academic Town (pop. 40,000) a location of choice for families who work or study there. Ten miles to the north stands Novosibirsk with population over 1.5 million and a subway under the river.

A central aim of those who planned this *Akademgorodok* was to facilitate a faster transfer of new knowledge between institutions of research and of learning. More recently, selected industries also have become part of this mix, for applying new knowledge directly to production. Many researchers in the institutes also teach in the university.

In recent decades the model has spread to other centers. Already in the 1980s, VUZy in Irkutsk and other locations in Siberia and the Far East were developing or planning their own versions of *Akademgorodok.*

Recent Adaptations.

Four Pivotal Policy Changes.

Since 1987, several policy changes occurred at the national level which ramified quickly through the system of Russian higher education and worked significant effects on VUZy in Pacific Russia. The following four proved pivotal.

(1) Rectors—i.e. the local VUZ administration—received broader authority over the academic program(s) of their institutions. Working with his or her institution's "Council of Scholars," the rector could now make changes as big as adding a new faculty (school) or closing a faltering one. At some point the central ministry would have a budgetary veto over big decisions, but this enhanced authority still set loose significant reform at the local level.

(2) No more "first job assignment"—The practice of mandatory "distribution" (*raspredeleniya*) or assignment of new graduates to their first jobs was abandoned. Students now, diploma in hand, had the responsibility and freedom to find their own employment. While this may appear to American students as an essential right, it proved terrifying to many students then "in the pipeline" of undergraduate studies in Pacific Russia. How to even find an appropriate job opening? How to find an apartment in a strange location, without family network? How to find an income for a spouse? These now became the individual's responsibilities.

This change had an energizing effect in the classroom, according to professors. "Previously, they knew they had to graduate," observes one grinning professor, "but now they know that they have to know something." In some fields, what partly took the place of the job assignment system is a system of three-way contracts, described elsewhere.

(3) Less financial support from central government—Whether by design or neglect, financial support from the central ministries in the 1990s declined precipitously. In either case it was a decision of budgetary policy. As Alaskans know, the costs of living farthest from the larger supply centers are higher. So the shortfall of support hit VUZy in Pacific Russia even harder than most other regions. In view of this decline, the government had no choice but to stand back as the VUZy themselves found new sources of support. So it did, and they did.

(4) Regional examination of scholars—The Russian federal accrediting commission (*attestatsionnaya commissia*) increasingly authorized selected VUZy to examine candidates for advanced scholarly degrees. Prior to that time, candidates for advanced degrees had to travel to Moscow to stand for examination and to defend their dissertations before a committee and audience most of whose members they didn't know. Now most candidates can remain in their own region for this career step. Among other effects, there's now less tendency to skim off the brightest and best by enticements to relocate to "the center" from "the provinces."

This shift of authority to the regions means that higher education in Pacific Russia has become more autonomous, and is judged capable to replenish its own supply of scholars and highly trained experts. It implies an acknowledgment at the center that the region has its own sufficient scholarship and expertise to cultivate and test new generations of scholars and experts in most disciplines. (See Chapter 4 for further discussion.)

To summarize these new policies: As early as 1987 the central government (first Soviet, then Russian) began to articulate numerous policy actions which affect VUZy in Pacific Russia, including the creation of a few new VUZy. The four changes sketched above enabled or set loose most of the changes that could be observed in individual VUZy over the following decade. We will return to three of them in further detail in the next chapter.

Early Effects on Students.

If you ask deans and prorectors for a comparison of today's students with students of five or eight years ago, it probably will evoke an animated discussion. Most agree that students currently take their studies more seriously than did their predecessors of the 1980s. "They have become responsible for their individual futures," said one dean. "Maybe too self-centered. They now must compete for jobs," not by currying favor inside their own familiar VUZ for a good "placement," but in the job market. And they now "know that they also must know something" in order to hold the job.

At some institutions, the competition for admission has increased significantly—one hears ratios of from two to seven applicants for each student seat. This varies by institution and by faculty (school/department) within each institution. A rector here and a prorector there have claimed with visible relief that they no longer feel obliged to pass students from year to year if they don't do satisfactory work. The VUZ now also has the power to manipulate its quotas for incoming class size. Thus it can induce competition and so raise the average competence level of the student body.

"Quota" here means the number of students to whom the government will pay stipends and for whom it also pays the VUZ. Local administrators may go beyond these quotas if they can find other sources of support, and they do. This also heightens temptations for corruption, and one hears increasingly of underqualified students being admitted for varying "fee" levels.

Sponsored students.

Another reason for the increased student seriousness lies in the 3-way contract system mentioned above. In this arrangement, an enterprise, business or government agency agrees to sponsor and pay for one or more students through all five undergraduate years; the student agrees to work for that firm for a specified minimum time (usually 3 to 5 years); and the VUZ agrees to provide specified education/training toward that goal. Some VUZy at first received a substantial percentage of enrollment by means of such contracts—30 percent or more. The numbers declined, however, as some enterprises faltered or fell. In any case, administrators and instructors tend to agree that such sponsored students, with a promised first job to prepare for, pursue their major studies steadily and with concentration. In some VUZy these contract-supported students now may comprise 10 percent of the total. Their numbers probably will grow again as regional production improves.

Still other students (or their parents) pay their own tuition. Moreover, tuition varies according to the field or specialty and so, apparently, do additional "fees."

For whatever reason, students now tend to have a more realistic view of the world of market economics. As mentioned above, when the '90s began students left VUZy in droves, hoping to make good incomes by their own pluck and new opportunities. Later they began to return to the VUZy or find other educational and training sources. By the mid-'90s many students were trying, American-style, to balance both a job and full-time study. Such students tend to be more methodical, more diligent learners, according to instructors.

Changes in Program and Curriculum.

Staying calm.

In the decade 1986–96, it is not much of an exaggeration to say that *everything* in Russia was either changing or up for decision. At first, relief and exhilaration, then wonderment and anxiety, then despair verging on fear marked conversations with academic people in Pacific Russia. Under such conditions, one might have expected bright youth to take to the streets or to retreat into comforting, private diversions. Instead, it is a striking phenomenon that students continued attending classes, helped with the fall harvest, chose their study majors, and tried to imagine personal futures such as their parents could not have anticipated. The VUZy proceeded with their daily business in deliberate ways, ways that outwardly did not flaunt the depth of change actually occurring.

Foreign languages.

In VUZy of Pacific Russia, changes quickly occurred in the foreign languages offered and the direction of interest in international relations. Given new opportunity, they turned toward the Pacific Rim. During Soviet times it was remarkable that Asian languages were listed as offered only at Far East State University (Vladivostok) or Leningrad State University. If you majored in one, you also had to study English. But now Japanese, Korean, and Chinese language instruction appeared in VUZy from Irkutsk to Khabarovsk. Individual VUZy are paying attention to the nature, needs and support of their own regions. In Chita, an oblast' with a long border on China, one high school had long taught Chinese, but that was not widely known outside Chita and its large border garrison.

For completeness it must be mentioned that the new pedagogical institute at Birobidjan, Jewish Autonomous Oblast', also offers **Yiddish language** (not Hebrew) among its majors. Originally, Stalin's regime hoped to attract speakers of Yiddish from European Russia to this frontier area. Now, ironically, Yiddish might expedite one's passage *from* here. Yet, at least, an old promise was fulfilled by this innovation.

Not ideologies, but perceived opportunities drove the new turn of curricula toward Pacific Rim interests. English language had long been one of the standard foreign languages offered in VUZy along with French and German (and sometimes Spanish). It was British English, and the textbooks reflected it. But the turn toward the Pacific changed that, and soon American-style English became a growth industry in the VUZy.

Pedagogical institutes with good **English language** departments, as in Irkutsk, Ulan Ude, and Khabarovsk, found themselves in new and increasing demand. Not that every prospective teacher wanted to teach this language after graduating, but students wanted the ability to work for an employer dealing with Americans, Canadians, Australians. To people in this region, the U.S. after all is the biggest player on the Pacific Rim. Why not China or Japan? People speak politely of these near neighbors, yet their historical sense—both past and future—inclines them toward Americans, Australians and Canadians as partners. Asian firms have made memorable blunders. Even in 1995 one advertised for young Russian women to work in Japan for six months as "hostesses," language not required! In addition, however, English language has become the *lingua franca,* the common language used even at meetings of Chinese, Koreans, and Japanese with Russians.

New international ties.

In the major VUZy of Pacific Russia, offices in charge of **international ties and programs** were created or enhanced. Scholars and administrators were thrilled by the prospect of reaching out to yet-unknown academic colleagues around the Pacific Rim. Administrators hoped that such offices could devise ways to bring in foreign students by contract, thus a new source of income. In the Far East, contingents of students from China (PRC) and Korea (ROK) soon arrived by contract. Although these visiting students tend not to mix with local students, Russian instructors teach them Russian language, culture and a technical specialty. Such groups do indeed provide new income and contacts for host VUZy.

Meanwhile, other initiatives enabled undergraduate students from Pacific Russian VUZy to study for a semester or full year at an American institution. Lewis & Clark College of Portland, Oregon was perhaps the first such host, beginning in the 1980s to receive groups of undergraduates from Khabarovsk State Ped. Institute in Portland's sister city. Later the American Council of Teachers of Russian (ACTR) launched a major nationwide competition under which selected leading undergraduates from Russia, including Pacific Russia, are placed in American universities each academic year. (ACTR also sponsors one of several programs for Russian high school youth to visit an American school.)

The "Tahoe-Baikal Project" represents yet another type of exchange involving students. While not exclusively for students, this project annually (1991-) selects a dozen young Russians and a dozen young Americans for a summer of work and study together. Each person selected must have a demonstrated interest and background in environmental protection. Together they spend a month at Lake Baikal and a month at Lake Tahoe. At both ends this project has university and research center support.

Growth of Pacific Rim savvy.

By the mid-1990's one could meet, in the VUZy of Pacific Russia, a significant number of students and instructors with personal experience in other countries on the Pacific Rim. Now not only for eminent scholars or influential administrators, the possibility finally became real for instructors and students to personally engage the world *across the nearest borders* on the east end of Russia—borders with China, Japan, Korea, Canada and the U.S.A. Parents in Khabarovsk and Yakutsk, already in 1992, could say to an American visitor with a gleam in their eye, "We ourselves will not likely visit America, but our children probably will." Nearly everyone in a VUZ, it now seems, knows someone who's "been there." So the real worldscape—the portion of the world within which one functions mentally—expanded for students in Pacific Russia by a great leap during this period.[5]

Computer science.

During this same period, computer science also enjoys new popularity and growing demand among students. IBM computer hardware has shown up increasingly in laboratories of educational institutions. In Khabarovsk, a new "lyceum" or elite high school opened in 1992, preparing bright children in computer use and English language. Equipment and instructors seemed, on repeated visits by an American observer, first class. Their first graduates enjoyed great success on entering university studies. Likewise, the computer laboratory at Khabarovsk State Tech. University, by 1994, had acquired state-of-the-art hardware, some new graduate assistantships, and appeared well abreast of its field. The Computer Research Institute has its own international program officer with good English language skills. Although by no means the norm, it is no longer unusual to find computers and computer games in private urban homes.

The subjects of market economics, business management and business administration.

This suddenly began to command attention—both from new students and from VUZ administrators anxious to sustain enrollments. Change was everywhere, it seems futile to inventory the various additions and changes in this field. Here are the types: (a) There are full-blown dual degree programs in partnership with an American university. (b) There are undergraduate majors in Economics, most of them new but some revised and spliced into established faculties—e.g. "*Economics of* Forest Industry and Wood Products." (c) There are whole programs operated parallel with established curricula in VUZy, even part of the regular instructional offerings of a VUZ but for a special fee. (d) There are new business management curricula (majors) in institutes which once specialized in the economics of the Soviet system. (e) There are American-sponsored, extension-like programs in applied business management, offered on site at established Russian VUZy. (f) There are commercial courses—from "computers in business operation" to "Dale Carnegie marketing skills"—offered with no reference to a VUZ.

Some of the visiting American lecturers arrive with no prior knowledge of Russian culture and no grasp of the current climate for business in Pacific Russia. Some of the on-site Russian instructors have had little or no formal opportunity to reorient their approach to current actual economic conditions in their country and region. Yet student demand is high.

Some U.S. and Canadian firms—an American cosmetics firm, for example—bring their new Russian retailers across the Pacific to North America for a brief period of training in marketing their products. While by any definition this is not higher learning, it does afford a firsthand view of a "mature" market culture and a first international exposure for a number of enterprising adults. Still unknown, however, is the extent of efforts by such companies to understand the market conditions to which their Russian "reps" must adapt. (*See Chapter 5.*)

In fall 1992 the Yakutsk State University inaugurated a new Department of the Economics of the Pacific Rim, thus openly suggesting the direction of future economic interests of the Republic of Sakha (Yakutia). The Irkutsk State Institute of Economics, still at the corner of Karl Marx and Lenin Streets, renovated its curriculum and has a sustained enrollment of over 5,000. It, too, now has an Office of International Programs close to the rector's office. From these examples one can infer that the spectrum of

44

current instruction and training in the general field of market economics is both wide and in continual motion.

As mentioned, the University of Alaska and the University of Maryland have formed partnership programs with Pacific Russian VUZy. Such programs culminate in the standard Russian five-year diploma plus an American business degree. They entail collaborative instruction by American and Russian instructors at the host (Russian) VUZ and a period of instruction at the American partner campus. Another project, run by Portland State University, provides training in business management at the Khabarovsk Institute of Economics and Law.

Journalism.

Far Eastern State University established its own new School of Journalism, including broadcast journalism. Its curriculum even includes Political Science, Economics, Ecology, and Sociology!

"Gumanitarnye"/liberal arts.

A host of other kinds of curricular change have occurred. The discipline of **Sociology**, while not widespread, has become accessible for study at the undergraduate level. The same is true for **Psychology** beyond its traditional pedagogical use (Ed. Psych.). The **former ideological core** subjects have undergone systematic change:

—"History of the Soviet Communist Party," for example, became "History of Russia";
—"Marxist-Leninist Philosophy" became a survey of philosophy;
—"Scientific Communism" became political science/"politology;"
—"Scientific Atheism" became "world religions."

"Culturology," which according to its professors is not anthropology, has joined the canon of social science disciplines. So, in principle, there now is a core of breadth courses or general education. A lack of published textbooks and materials may still limit the effect of these changes, but the core is in place. (*See Appendix B regarding Russian term "gumanitarnye."*)

"Elective" courses.

For an undergraduate, these still appear in the major field (fourth and fifth years) rather than as opportunities to explore outside one's field (as, for example, a science major taking a fine arts course).

Environmental education also has entered the typical VUZ curriculum, but seldom as an academic major or specialization. (*See Chap. 4.*)

Higher education in comparison—the first postsecondary degree.

In contrast to the American bachelor of arts and bachelor of science degrees, which were designed as pre-professional degrees, Soviet VUZy offered standard five-year programs for *first professional* degrees which led directly into a professional job. To a large extent Russian VUZy continue this pattern. A school teacher's certification to teach, for instance, comes with the diploma, and an engineer graduates with license in hand. While it takes longer than five years to become a physician, medical education also begins directly after high school—there is not a "pre-med" program. For most fields the specialist's *diplom* requires five years of residential study (full-time, day) beyond eleven years of public school. (This discussion deliberately excludes trade school education and training.) Many (up to 50 percent) use the option of six years of evening attendance or extramural learning.

One must not woodenly compare/contrast these five years with America's "four-year" baccalaureate. Although the bachelor's is the nearest U.S. equivalent (and takes five or more years in current practice) in most cases, the *diplom* typically represents more advanced instruction in the specialization. On the other hand, the American bachelor's degree typically represents a wider spectrum of learning. Graduates of American liberal arts colleges will remember deans' speeches explaining to them why, in a democracy, they must gain an introductory knowledge of disciplined inquiry into every division of human learning—natural sciences, "hard" or pure sciences, social sciences, humanities, and basic communication. Today, however, observers seem more inclined to value the adaptability which that kind of breadth encourages, as technology accelerates change. Among educators, some Russians are pushing toward greater diversity and breadth in the curriculum, while many Americans want to narrow theirs to the requirements of a job. Even though both American and Russian systems continue to evolve and experiment, each one still reflects

46

its historic purpose. (*See page 51 below* on new Russian experiments with "*bakalavr*" baccalaureate structure.)

Life as an Undergraduate.

The new first-year student, having gained admission to a particular *fakul'tet* (school/division) within the VUZ, is assigned to a group of his/her peers who have chosen the same specialty. In general, this student will spend the next five years attending classes and undertaking various chores (e.g. preparing dormitories for occupancy, sealing windows for the winter, helping with the harvest) together with the others in this group. They will have a good chance of getting through and receiving their *diplom* together, since attrition remains low as compared to most American universities. Students, on entering, are generally seventeen years old. But it must be pointed out that in most VUZy up to half of the total enrollment count are students in evening or extramural divisions. These take longer to finish and may also enter at somewhat older ages.

A large majority of students come from urban homes, reflecting the mostly urban population of Pacific Russia today. Some come from villages or distant cities, and most VUZy have dormitories, cafeterias and other student accommodations. Indeed, one technical university maintains a student spa or health center, where for low cost a student (regardless of where his/her home is) may elect to live for five to six weeks while attending classes. Here the student can receive therapeutic massages, mineral baths, special diet and other types of individual care for personal health maintenance. The Maritime Academy has an impressive fleet of small boats for student recreational use. Another VUZ has its own campground on a year-round saltwater bay. Some students find employment there as camp staff—waitresses, etc.—for specified short periods. On campus there are student clubs, even for those wanting to hear visiting political speakers. Often on weekend nights there are dances and concerts. So although the Komsomol branches faded away when the CPSU did, students still have access to a diversity of extracurricular and social activities.

Classes and credits.
The typical undergraduate can expect to spend from 25 to 35 hours in class per week—a decrease from Soviet times! The class hour is defined as

45 minutes, and common practice schedules two such periods back-to-back, called a *para* (pair), for a class meeting of 90 minutes or less. There is no accounting system of "semester units" such as the Carnegie credit unit, and hours in laboratory, seminar, or practice count the same as in lecture-discussion. The curricular plan does not chop each subject into neat, semester-length courses—some are shorter, many longer than a one- or two-semester sequence.

No T.A.s

Teaching is by regular members of the instructional staff; there are almost no graduate *teaching* assistants, although some have been found in language faculties. Class sections generally are smaller, approximately half the average size of those in public American universities, and the student-instructor ratio is approximately twice as rich.

Exams.

There are quizzes which become part of an instructor's grade record, but most **end-of-course examinations still are oral.** In finals week each student takes a turn, stands individually before the instructor and one or two other professors, and responds orally to three questions given to him on a "ticket" shortly before he is summoned. From Russians one can hear many tales of deliberate grade-skewing by instructors in this oral exam process. But in Pacific Russia, motives ascribed to such instructors are not likely to be ethnic/nationality motives, as they are in western Russia. In an interview, one rector in Vladivostok grinned that his VUZ had administered a *written final* examination in mathematics, and both students and instructors had found it more challenging.

"Course paper" grades are recorded separately on the student's transcript. If the class sequence hasn't ended by the end of a given semester, the instructor may simply give a "Pass" or "Credit" (*zachyot*) until the time does arrive for a final examination.

Students from the third year onward typically have to write at least one "year's paper" (two-semester paper), and a "graduation paper" or senior thesis. In general, the student in Pacific Russia has fewer writing assignments, fewer papers requiring library research or other kinds of independent inquiry than in American colleges. At the same time it seems that more in-class recitation occurs, but this observation comes from only anecdotal evidence. In any case, recitation amounts must vary by discipline. (*Note: Typically, Russians comparing the two systems do not know how heavily American instructors rely on written assignments which are carefully critiqued and written tests of both essay and "objective" variants. Also seldom realized: many departments in American colleges require a "senior thesis"—similar to the VUZ' graduation project—for graduating.)*

Comparing creature comforts a student from Novosibirsk visiting an American VUZ exclaimed, "If only we had it so good at my VUZ! . . . !" Yet the student in eastern Russia experiences less loneliness, less isolation than the typical American undergraduate. The cultural habits of dependence on one's long-term group have roots in Russia preceding the Soviet-Communist era. Today, a student in, say, Khabarovsk who very rationally savors his growing autonomy still turns to peers in class for an answer when stumped by a question from the instructor. He does not regard this as cheating, but as the normal way of finding an answer that he does not individually know. American managers looking for "cooperative problem-solving" should take note of this factor in the student culture.

Figure 4 helps to summarize this comparison of student experience in U.S. and Pacific Russian VUZy.

Fig. 4: The Undergraduate Experience in Pacific Russia and Pacific U.S.A.

	Russian (Pacific region)	U.S.A. (Pacific coast)
1. Access to higher education.	Russia and U.S. both high in percentage of population with higher education, providing equal access by qualified youth, compared with European nations.	
2. Financial support for students	Formally, stipend and complete support from government for budgeted quota of students. Others now admitted by contract, and by "private payment."	Combination includes loans, grants, merit scholarships, job leads. Recent trend to reduce federal aid; California aid based on family income, student's need.
3. Financial support to institutions	Central ministries lag inflation rate, salary funds 3 months late, leads to unusual corruption. Finding local sources.	State gov't. reducing support, private sources increasing, sense of public uninterest, but alumni contributing.

Fig. 4: The Undergraduate Experience in Pacific Russia and Pacific U.S.A.

	Russian (Pacific region)	**U.S.A. (Pacific coast)**
4. Aim of first diploma	Professional specialty and rank.	Pre-professional; introduction to inquiry in each field of knowledge.
5. Peer support system	Advance w/same group of classmates (20–24) through five years.	Finding compatible peer group is major personal/individual task.
6. Role in shaping own program	After choice of specialty (fakul'tet / school), there are few electives, though increasing.	Many decisions and electives, especially defining individual major. (30%)
7. In-class load	25–35 class hours per week. One class hour is 45 minutes, often in back-to-back pairs. No different weight for lecture, lab., practice hours.	12–18 lecture hours per week (labs more). 1 class hour=50 minutes. Different credit value for lecture, lab., practice hours.
8. Papers/Reports	Year-end paper required for years 3–5; graded separately on transcript; + graduation paper defended in person/audience.	Many one-semester courses include "term paper." Typical student has three term papers per semester and a "senior project."
9. Home work (outside assignments)	Most assignments prepare for recitation.	Most assignments are for writing, "short paper."
10. Help in class recitation	Peer help is normal, though illicit.	Peer help may be penalized; is forbidden and uncommon.
11. Examinations	Most are oral, to instructors, at end of course.	Most are written, graded by one. At end of each semester.

Fig. 4: The Undergraduate Experience in Pacific Russia and Pacific U.S.A.

	Russian (Pacific region)	U.S.A. (Pacific coast)
12. Community involvement	September may be spent helping in regional harvest; length of semester can vary.	Much volunteer work in community; all courses fit standard semester length regardless.
13. Urban/Rural	Large majority are urban, reflecting population. Age 18 to 24.	Diverse, reflecting population. Less prestigious VUZy have a higher average age of students—over 25.
14. Student employment	Many students now have outside job.	Most students work 20 or more hours per week for income.
15. Dress	Most students dress "up" as for professional position.	Many dress "down"; slovenly is still in style.
16. Change major	Difficult to change major outside one's school/fakul'tet.	Common to change major at least once, across academic fields, delaying graduation.
17. Length of program to degree	Most require five years for full-time, day students.	Officially four to five years; most actually use five years, take more than minimum requirements.
17-A Grad. study	Few places, but increasing at many VUZy; no T.A.s.	Many spaces, some helping with instruction or research.
18. Job entry	Professional "license" comes with diploma.	Professional school and licensure are further hurdles beyond diploma.

(Table not to be copied for distribution without written permission—D.M. Heckman)

51

Experiments with Structure and Time to Degree.

With more local authority by the end of the '80s, VUZy began to experiment with different patterns, e.g. a baccalaureate followed by a master's degree program. In 1995, however, the federal Committee for Higher
Education issued official minimum standards for higher professional education. They stipulate that, where a program offers a baccalaureate, the
minimum timespan must be 4 years after secondary school. They aim to
make degrees more portable internationally. (Source: *Gosudarstvennyi
obrazovatel'nyi standart vyshshego professional'nogo obrazovaniya;*
Komitet Rossiskoi federatsii po vysshemu obrazovaniyu, Moskva 1995.)
The aim is *not to mimic* the current American pattern of baccalaureate programs, but to take due account of the benefits of (a) greater breadth of subject matter in the typical American bachelor's curriculum, and (b) greater
personal responsibility of U.S. undergraduates for decisions about their
program.

East Siberian Technological Institute (now University), Ulan Ude,
began in 1993 to offer new students the option of a four-year track to a
bachelor of science in engineering. If qualified, one could follow that with
two more years to a master of science degree. By 1996, reportedly more
than twenty percent of each entering class opted for the bachelor's (*bakalavr*) route. The chief problem, however, was that this B.S. degree does not
qualify the student for licensure as an engineer. The faculty was engaged in
hot debate about the value of the new option.

Student Uses of the Institution.

In eastern Russia today just as in America, students manage to make
their own uses of VUZy other than uses intended by the planners or administrators. Some graduates of an institute for training builders of rail systems, for example, never work in the railroad industry, but apply their
knowledge to construction of apartment houses and office buildings. Now
they might work in the communications industry.

Perhaps the most widespread examples of this occur in student uses of
pedagogical institutes. In 1992–93 the salaries of school teachers, because
of an inability to keep up with the rate of inflation, were worse than ever;
yet the competition *increased* for admission into the pedagogical institute

faculties of foreign languages, *continuing a recent trend of increased competition and growth.* This was especially so for the English language major. That is perceived by students as a rather direct route into new enterprises and the commercial world, especially into some form of Pacific Rim business. It is a fact, also, that many elected legislators and other public officials in Pacific Russia today are graduates of pedagogical institutes/teachers colleges. As the most widespread form of VUZ, the teacher's colleges of Siberia/Far East seem positioned to function as student conduits into a new entrepreneurial and democratic order. Yet, as some technical institutes aggressively promote new programs in economics and management, they too enter the competition to speed the transition taking place in their city and region. Institutional survival demands branching far afield.

Regionalizing Higher Education.

As mentioned elsewhere, not only do students make their own uses of available programs, but also academic administrators at the local level search for and sometimes find ways to adapt their VUZy to regional economic needs which may diverge from the original assigned mission of their institution. Two illustrations will suffice.

(a) The new pedagogical institute in Birobidjan considers adding an Agronomy Faculty to train farmers because the oblast', predominantly agricultural, has no other VUZ to serve that need.

(b) Yakutsk State University wanted to find a way to prepare permanent residents of Yakutia (Sakha) for dealing professionally in "international economic relations." As an autonomous republic of the RF, Yakutia wants the right to turn its own economic affairs and to contract with foreign entities. So its university in 1992 planted a new program as a Chair (*kafedra*) of Pacific Economic Relations within the School (*facul'tet*) of Mathematics, at least temporarily. Here there had been flagging enrollment, and here also was a ready structure which could conclude an official agreement with the School of Business, University of Alaska. Through that agreement, students who complete a five-year program of study in the new Department of International Economic Relations can receive both a regular *diplom* from Yakutsk State University *and* a Bachelor of Business Administration from the University of Alaska.

Earlier mention was made of the opening of Asian languages in VUZy in areas bordering on Asian countries and the trend toward American English here in the part of Asia nearest to San Francisco. All these represent a trend toward the VUZy "regionalizing" themselves. Such moves, of course, stand to benefit the VUZy as well as their regions. Financial survival demands that these VUZy now turn increasingly toward the major enterprises and governments of their own regions and cities for support. (*See Chapter 3.*) In at least two large territories, rectors confided that some local public support had begun, but they regard this as such a tender matter that they requested confidentiality. As the VUZy continue to engage managers and public administrators in dialog about their highly prepared human resource needs, and as graduates continue to move into significant leadership in Pacific Russia, the VUZy will increasingly be seen as organic parts of the life and economy of their own communities.

Still Too Rosy? A Self-Critique.

Nearly all the information in this chapter, unless another source has been cited, comes from interviews, firsthand observations and data gathered by the author during extended visits to Pacific Russia beginning in 1986. To some readers it will seem too positive to fit past or current reports, too optimistic or even "rosy." First, academic professionals make their living in part by analytical critique and proposing possible flaws in a presentation. Others, no matter their age, have heretofore only negative images of Russian institutions in Siberia and "the eastern provinces," or have dealt with Russians who themselves lack current knowledge of some changes. Who can blame them? So, honest skepticism deserves a complex response.

(a) Much has changed since the 1980s in Pacific Russia, as in the Russian Federation overall, and VUZy continue to change although in ways more individual than before. This individuating makes it more difficult to generalize now than when all VUZy and each program had to conform to a single plan. It also becomes more perilous to base critique on observations from a different region or a different decade. This in itself is positive!

(b) There's "enough ignorance to go around." Americans and other outsiders for a half century received woefully inadequate information and impressions about that end of Russia nearest to Seattle and San Francisco.

If a journalist visited Siberia (1948–85), it generally was via Moscow to the coal-mining villages in western Siberia or reindeer herders in rural areas that would make a good story, perhaps arranged by a friendly Moscow official. If a western photographer visited a city in Pacific Russia, he might show the monotonous nine-story apartment houses (*"Khruscheviki"*) built everywhere without landscaping to solve the housing problem; the photographer probably would not know that this ugly phenomenon reflected a rush to the cities similar to America in the 1920s. Nor would the reportage point out that Siberian cities had no homeless people. (In the 1990s this changed as refugees arrived from the Caucasus.) The degree of urbanization in Pacific Russia surprises even Muscovites. Regarding higher education institutions, Russians and Americans alike tend to confuse "prestige of institution" with "quality of learning." So a VUZ in the "farthest provinces" (this language is used) would not immediately command the same respect as it would if it were located in Moscow or St. Petersburg.

(c) In the VUZy themselves, there remain endless details one can criticize. Many local academics (who tend to idealize American university conditions even while discounting the level of U.S. undergraduate knowledge) feel defensive about discussing concrete problems. Others unload endlessly about the terrible (*uzhasnoe*) conditions. In many or even most VUZy, physical facilities may resemble those of America's historical black colleges in the 1960s. Most classroom chalkboards need replacing and most restrooms need renovating. Library collections lag seriously by American standards, as they do in many *American* libraries now! Concerning faculty pay, more will be said later. But there seems little to gain from the age-old academic game of "Ain't it awful." That game and other life in the VUZy goes on.

(d) The author has taught for a full six months in two different VUZy. He has discussed "process" questions with instructors and deans at two dozen VUZy in seven different cities of Pacific Russia. Moreover he has talked with Russian students visiting U.S. institutions. From all this it is fair to conclude that life in the VUZy, including internal political game-playing, proceeds in a robust manner.

(e) The present findings result from academic research, not from detective investigation into illegal activities. One *assumes* some level of illegal activity where human beings gather, and especially where they gather under conditions of personal financial crisis. One hears of parents who give special pay-offs to get daughters and sons into a university and thus avoid seeing them drafted for military service and sent to Chechnya. One hears of "official transcripts and diplomas" purchased in Moscow subway or in the office of a dean's secretary. Yet it remains the primary aim of this monograph to provide *new descriptive information and analysis rather than in-depth critique*. Obviously, critique can come only after adequate descriptive information.

(f) During the final days of writing this monograph, economic conditions in Russia were deteriorating rapidly. Even by publication time, conditions in VUZy may force even more extreme change (e.g. closure) than reported here. Yet, in view of decades of the politics of negative critique, on each side toward the other, it may provide a useful corrective to focus on positive changes being made by VUZy in the face of both political and financial crisis.

Current Questions and Issues.

New Student Profile?

In a book entitled *An Objective Necessity— . . . Reforming Russian Higher Education (Ob'yektivnaya neobkhodimost')*, Moscow 1995, V.G. Kinelev addressed questions that Americans would discuss under "liberal education" (*gumanitarnoe obrazovanie*). Kinelev was chairman of the Federal Committee on Higher Education, holds a doctorate and the rank of professor in the Russian system. He recognizes that, in the present world context, significant problems often have a complexity that requires complex understanding—knowledge from diverse fields. A problem may have a logical and technical solution, but *solutions* will fail if not tempered by understanding and insights from, for example, the social sciences.

Today's student, Kinelev argues, needs a broader, multi-field education—i.e. liberal arts. In the student's near future there will come situations requiring broader understanding and greater flexibility than what is now normally provided through the five-year specialist's degree program (or the ensuing first scholarly degree, the *Kandidat nauk*—Auth.).

Kinelev also calls for greater attention to the moral and spiritual development of students—a theme which recurs predictably from one generation to the next. For this he proposes a greater role in the curriculum for disciplines which, in America, are grouped together as "liberal arts." As always, this raises a question of whether—and to what extent—human behavior is changed or affected by instruction, by rational discourse. Kinelev does not explore opportunities to change the affective side of a Russian student's experience, i.e. outside the classroom. Yet he does reflect broad concerns about flexibility in Russian students.

It should not detract from the force of Kinelev's argument to mention that much of his argument already was made by Russian educators in 1987. In 1987 the central government issued a major new policy statement, *"Osnovnie napravleniya perestroiki vysshego obrazovaniya v stranie"* (Basic Guidelines for Rebuilding Higher Education in the Nation). The politics changed since then, but many of the same educators remained influential. Some general directions of "rebuilding" had thus begun before Kinelev's book.

Kinelev calls for, among other things,

> formation in future specialists (graduates of VUZy) of a high level of general and professional culture, a *capability to adapt oneself dynamically to new conditions* of the daily life of a society based in market economy (p. 158).

The term "dynamically" here means, not only an ability to change once, but ongoing flexibility for shifting judiciously with a world in which change is ongoing and not always in predicted directions.

Thus the question of student characteristics—the profile of the principal "product" of higher education institutions in Russia—is again being discussed at the highest levels. The first prorector of a VUZ in Khabarovsk directed the attention of the present author to Kinelev's book, indicating that administrators in Pacific Russia also are discussing this question. Perhaps regional leaders in the commercial realm, therefore, will find ways to participate in determining the new shape of highly educated human resources in Pacific Russia.

Changing Effects of Chronic Financial Stress—1992–96.

In East Siberia and the Russian Far East, higher education lives! But hungrily. Financial stress, both institutional and individual/personal, continues to take its grinding toll. Because of the rapid pace of changes engulfing Russia in the 1990s, it seems useful to record here some impressions of

VUZy in eastern Russia first in 1992–93 and then again in 1995–96 as institutions and individuals in them struggled to maintain equilibrium.

In 1992–93, rectors, some of them newly elected and others reaffirmed by councils of their institutions, expressed wrenching concern about the *salary levels* of their teaching staff, mostly due to runaway inflation. Yet they also told with enthusiasm of recent academic reforms and future plans. These did not sound like ship captains thinking about abandoning their craft. Deans spoke in even tones about problems, such as maintaining adequate faculties, yet they told also about recent improvements and present hopes. In a few places, conversation revealed significant personal depression, but people also retained a dignity and even a sense of humor about the challenges.

At the departmental level, some professors and instructors displayed anxiety and pessimism, mostly because of the inflation eating up substantial wage increases. Other concerns, such as internal politics (i.e. within the institution) and attrition entered their conversation. Yet others were upbeat about a recent promotion or the raise just announced (Sept. '92). Students poured out of classrooms and into animated conversations in hallways; young women dressed neatly, even fashionably, their male classmates often in western-style denims. Students and instructors usually appeared at ease in talking with one another, and an American visitor would be startled at the frequency with which students can interrupt a dean.

Most facilities are, by American standards, poor or at least drab-looking—but not all. Some VUZy have acquired new dormitories in the past five years, others have completed renovation of a classroom building. Diverse capital construction was visibly progressing. University of Yakutsk (end of 1996) moved its faculties of Biology, Geography and Chemistry into a grand new 6-story structure complete with indoor climate-controlled gardens. Far Eastern State University added a new building for social sciences and languages, while other VUZy underwent major renovations. One must remember, however, that the model for most Russian university facilities is the European urban model, not the rural British/American "campus."

Attrition remained small, by American standards, although it has caused some unwanted displacement of academic departments. *The student-faculty ratio overall improved, and would make most American academics envious.* Competition among students for admission to certain "faculties"—i.e. academic divisions—and other factors tended to improve

New "corpus" for Schools of Biology, Chemistry, and Geography, Yakutsk State University, Sakha (Yakutia), northeast Russia. 1996.

Layout of botanical garden with climate control, inside new corpus, Yakutsk State University. 1996.

the quality of the new student classes, according to comments by several faculty members.

So a dispassionate but interested visitor in 1992–93 could not avoid the impression of newly released energy in response to the increased local autonomy and other new conditions, as well as new problems. In view of those problems, the foregoing impressions sounded too optimistic to some. Yet those impressions came from many actual encounters.

By 1995–96, one could feel in the long-established VUZy less optimism and more of a sense of need to "hold onto the day job" while foraging for the rest of one's financial support. A renowned and respected professor of foreign languages excused herself early to travel across town to the new private institution where she and a few colleagues realize extra income from teaching the children of some of the "new Russians" (newly rich) in town. Another recruits her American interviewer to give lectures to a private tutorial group and immediately hurries off to tend to yet another income-producing enterprise. A professional woman marvels aloud that her professor–father recently constructed a family dacha—a sudden necessity for their family food supply. Carpentry is not his hobby nor pastime. He already fills two university teaching positions and one administrative post. An able computer professor suddenly disappears on a "business trip" (*komandirovka*) for a month of the semester. On returning, he confides only that the *leave* was a financial necessity—evidently some kind of moonlighting opportunity. The administrative assistant to a dean, in planning an office party, asks an honored guest to bring fresh fruit instead of the traditional floral bouquet; fresh fruit has become a rarity in her household.

With such extra foraging for a living by many academic professionals, a visitor to a VUZ at the height of a semester can feel like a visitor in an American college during the week before Christmas. Everyone seems engaged in important business somewhere else unnamed and "will return soon, maybe before the end of the workday." All during 1995–96 salary funds from the central government arrived three (or more) months late. When the funds finally did arrive, instructors generally did not know what amount they could expect to receive—regular increases did not seem to catch up with the rate of inflation, and within a given VUZ the *rektorat* (president's office) may have changed the proportions of the salaries by rank. (*See examples of faculty pay scale for Fall 1995, in Chap. 3.*)

Summary.

This chapter has outlined not only the *scope* of higher education in Pacific Russia today, but also the general nature of its *dynamic change* during the tumultuous transition of Russian society that began with the Gorbachev government. Higher education here, it can be said, has made a great leap forward, though not without pain. Institutions (VUZy), gaining greater autonomy, have become entrepreneurial and more attuned to the economic needs of their own region. They have grown in number and variety, maybe in spirit of competition with one another. And they have projected themselves eastward, engaging firmly with colleagues on the Pacific Rim including the U.S.A. and Canada. All this has been accompanied by striking changes in curricula as well as changes in the profile of the "typical student."

The next chapter will elaborate somewhat on effects of three of the four policy changes described here, provide illustrative data on faculty salaries, and offer brief sketches of several VUZy and their participation in the economic transition. Readers interested only in economic and human resource issues may choose to continue directly to Chapter 4.

Notes

1. During the Cold War, the U.S., too, had official doubts about the "loyalty" of such western scholars who could find ways to cross Pacific boundaries. When students formally invited him, Farley Mowat (a Canadian citizen) was prohibited by the U.S. government from travelling to Sacramento to lecture on his 1970s adventures visiting Siberia. "He must have had Communist Party connections," they reasoned, "so we can't let him in to talk on a university campus." Mowat is a naturalist, author of *Never Cry Wolf* and other observations of life in far northern latitudes.
2. "Traditional" in the historical sense of universities; not "applied" or "professional training" except for the academic profession of research and teaching.
3. Source: "Goskomstat Rossii" (Russian Federal Committee on Statistics), 1993.
4. Evidently these figures count only those graduating from the VUZy in the region/area named.
5. Of the ten families that have hosted the author since 1992, eight of the parents and six of the children had visited the U.S. by the end of 1998, each for five weeks or longer duration.

3

New Powers, New Problems, New Initiatives of Higher Educational Institutions

Since 1987, changes both planned and unplanned by the central government have combined to make higher educational institutions (VUZy) more entrepreneurial than anyone likely imagined up to that time. The previous chapter, outlining the scope of higher education in eastern Russia, also listed recent changes of policy by Moscow regarding higher education. This chapter will elaborate on certain of those changes.

The following three policy changes by the central Russian government seem fundamental because each one ramifies—i.e. leads to further changes—through the system:

1. Authority and responsibility for VUZy have been redistributed, resulting in greater autonomy for each VUZ, and producing simpler lines of connection to the central government;
2. Financial support by central government for VUZy has been severely diminished;
3. The practice of *raspredelenie*—assignment of 5th year students to particular jobs upon their graduation from the VUZ as "specialists"—has ceased.

While other changes could be mentioned, let us see how these three branch out and affect the system.

Policy change (A): Greater autonomy, simpler ties to "the center."

It is tempting to recall the old folk-saying of the *promyshlenniki,* the frontiersmen of Russian companies on the Pacific in the 19th century, when they felt confronted by a new legal or moral choice: "God is in His heaven, and the Czar is far, far away." For, among native Siberians even today, there remains a certain marked spirit of self-reliance when conditions press for it. In the early 1990s, conditions for operating a VUZ changed so abruptly and regularly as to evoke something of that spirit in academic leaders.

The policy of making each VUZ more flexible and more responsible for its own decisions did not appear suddenly from nowhere after the break-up of the USSR. The 1987 policy statement alluded to above, *Basic Guidelines for Restructuring Higher Education in the USSR*, already made reference to providing greater decision-making authority to each local rector of an institution, and discussed ways to enable each VUZ to adapt itself better to actual economic and technological conditions. But at last in 1991–92, after several other efforts, the government of the Russian Federation (RF) declared that a VUZ is essentially autonomous under the law, guided by its own "scholars' council" and not to be interfered with by organs of government.[1] As everyone knew then, Moscow still held all the financial strings.

To trace in detail the numerous shifts of power at the "center"—several changes of government between 1987 and 1993, structural changes of ministries, etc.—could distract from discerning the trend—a decentralizing of academic authority, "bucking it down" increasingly to the level of the individual VUZ. This trend continued from 1987 onward.

Decisions, for example, about what actual content to offer in place of abandoned ideological courses, or about additional new courses, new departments, faculty appointments—these and other issues certainly are tempered by thoughts about the next accreditation visit, but they commonly are resolved around the desk of a rector/academic council within an institution. When one VUZ in the Far East, for example, signed a written agreement with a California university to exchange a limited number of students and mutually waive tuition for that purpose, the Russian rector needed no higher authority to endorse it. Indeed some new international programs evidently can be authorized at the prorector (v.pres.) level.

At the same time, authority within a Russian VUZ remains more concentrated than in an American public university. One clue to this lies in the time required for gaining approval for some new initiative. A Russian dean of engineering invited colleagues from the U.S. to an international conference at his institution, to convene in Summer '93. He could not provide precise details—dates, agenda, reg. fee—until late March '93. When no American academic engineers responded, this dean could not understand why they would need more time to secure funds and to schedule such travel. The top-down command system still prevails even at the local level, and makes some things happen faster. Within the overall budget, a rector can even vary the faculty pay scale. (*See Table 5, page 77.*)

Russian higher education has no tradition of academic tenure for professors. All appointments—at least for classroom teaching positions—come up for reconsideration every five years, *within* the VUZ. In at least one major VUZ, the administration has shifted everyone to a one-year renewable contract basis. In others, "contract" seems to be a strange concept. Such conditions, of course, mitigate against much accumulation of power by the instructional staff scholars. Cases in Pacific Russia are known, nevertheless, where one or more professors took prominent part in civic protest demonstrations in the 1990s and still retained their jobs. Yet one can confidently argue that local VUZ authority remains concentrated at the top.

Of course, even with concentrated authority, not all changes in VUZy occur neatly, without delays or frayed egoes. It took some ministries longer than others to accept and understand their reduced authority over VUZy in their sector of the economy. In October '92 the rector of a ped. institute (pedagogical college) commented with several other officers present that he had received a certain directive from one ministry and was about to comply, when on the next day he received a contrary directive from the other ministry that shared authority over his institution. He grinned about the relative freedom which such ambiguity implied for an alert rector. Also, of course, some rectors are more open than others to delegating authority. So the transfer of academic power has not followed a uniform course in all VUZy.

Policy change (B.): Eroded financial support from Moscow.

Some will correctly point out that major funding of higher education everywhere in the Russian Federation still flows from "the center"—Moscow. Not only general salary funds for staff and faculty, but also student stipends, capital funds for constructions and renovation, and a per-student formula of support for the institution itself continues to come from Moscow. The tax structure itself has remained centralized, so also has the control over most public funds. Directly related to the allocation of public support, the process of *attestatsia*—government accreditation of individual VUZy—remains a central function. So it is true that certain pivotal powers over higher education in Pacific Russia are vested in Moscow. Still, more authority and more responsibility have been placed on each VUZ itself. Therefore individuation of these institutions proceeds apace. That is to say, it is becoming less and less feasible to predict the actual program of a VUZ in eastern Russia simply on the basis of a central "model" in or near Moscow. Greater variation is developing by region and by perceptions of local need—an academic marketplace.

Along with increased local authority, there also came a decrease in actual funds provided from the center. Correction: *Substantial increases from the center fell woefully behind the rate of inflation of the ruble, so they actually functioned as decreases.*

The rector of a diverse and respected university, Irkutsk State, in October 1993 said with visible anguish that senior professors—outstanding in their fields, he stressed—now were receiving less than 30 percent of the income level of carpenters. His new authority to set and vary the salaries of faculty members had become maddeningly constricted by the size of the allocation his institution actually received. That total allocation had just increased by a large number of rubles, but inflation had galloped ahead of the increase. Whether by policy decision or by default, the university had been left to fend for its own additional funds for survival. This perception was shared widely among academic persons interviewed in fall, 1993, and continuing through 1996.

In fall, 1995 the salary scale at two of the largest VUZy in the Russian Far East listed the following monthly amounts:

Table 5: Monthly Pay Scale at Two Higher Educational Institutions, Fall 1995

	VUZ #1	VUZ #2
Professor	1,806,848 Rubles	1,754,208 Rubles
Assoc. Prof.	1,003,200	1,359,168
Sr. Instructor	413,760	691,200
Instructor	323,500	562,848

These rates continued in force through 1996. *In mid-autumn, 1995 the official exchange rate, Russian rubles to U.S. was 4,640 rubles to one dol-*

lar. In 1996 it rose to 5430 rubles to one dollar. So, one can readily see that the two lower ranks of instructors could not pay all living expenses on their salaries (ranging from $60 to $127 per month). Not all living expenses, as of 1995, were comparable to the U.S. range. Housing was much less, so was local transportation, bread prices were still controlled. But food and clothing prices had become comparable to those in Portland, Sacramento and Seattle.[2]

At Yakutsk, where cost of living is nearly the highest in the country, the university pay scale was as follows:

Table 6: Monthly Pay Scale at Yakutsk State University, Yakutia/Sakha, Fall 1995

Professor	2,546,390 Rubles
Assoc. Prof.	1,947,742 Rubles
Sr. Instructor	1,176,120 Rubles
Instructor	886,777 Rubles

One medical school in Pacific Russia, meanwhile, reported the following scale.

Table 7: Monthly Pay Scale at a Medical School in Pacific Russia, Fall 1995

	Theoret/Academic Division	Clinical Division
Professor	1,522,088 Rubles	1,815,368 Rubles
Assoc. Prof.	1,036,200 Rubles	1,300,200 Rubles
Sr. Instructor	760,790 Rubles	—
Instructor	652,620 Rubles	1,048,620 Rubles

As becomes evident from such figures, when converted into equivalent US dollars all these academic pay rates amount to a few hundred dollars or less, per month.

Yet even these low salary rates were only numbers on paper. For the actual money to pay them was not arriving, or came three months late, or less than 100 percent arrived! By autumn, 1996 the mood of faculty members and administrators had slipped noticeably from bemused tolerance to angry desolation. They had joined the ranks of the newly poor, neglected by the Moscow government. They continued showing up at their offices and classrooms. Yet, on what were they to live?

For the academic profession enduring this new poverty, it could bear no resemblance at all to an armed siege of their city or to a national famine, which they could all suffer together and, together, work to overcome. No, in this case they must see their poverty in contrast to new and ostentatious wealth of other Russians nearby. They can see every day the clusters of new mansions in and around the city, generally built of brick and sometimes featuring a corner turret or other storybook architecture. They see gorgeous and expensive food items—e.g. imported whole pineapples for about $15—in the market and know that some neighbors, somehow, are buying them. In fact, they recognize some of the newly wealthy as their former students, and realize that for some there is little correlation between intelligence or talent and their new wealth. Here, in this region of the brave new market economy, the growing income gap phenomenon has arrived—poor getting poorer, and the intelligentsia—newly poor.

Under such conditions corruption is bound to grow, although our evidence for that serious claim here remains anecdotal. A report on National Public Radio (2 Nov. '97) told a current story of one family in Moscow that includes all essential elements of other personal tales we have heard on Russia's Pacific end. A substantial gift to someone involved in the admissions process of a VUZ. Admission to a VUZ seen by males as THE alternative to military conscription, truly life-threatening. Matter-of-fact bribery of key instructors at final examination time. In the NPR story, the student in a dental school paid a fixed rate of 300 U.S. dollars per examination (final exams are usually oral). Similar stories have come from personal sources about VUZy in the Caucasus. Although the nationality-ethnicity of a student again has become a factor in VUZy of western and southern Russia, we have not yet heard that this has shown up in Pacific Russia.

New Sources of Support.

The new financial pressure accelerated VUZy efforts to find new sources of support. Their new explorations, interestingly, have drawn some VUZy into much more dynamic, cooperative relations with the enterprises and governments of their own region and urban center. Five principal kinds of financial support, beyond allocations from Moscow, emerged.

1. Contracts.

The first additional source is the enterprise which plans to hire students who graduate from a VUZ. "Enterprise" here can mean any employer, from a large industrial complex to a relatively small company, or local or regional government. It includes a wide range of entities that depend upon specialists—college graduates—with higher level training for intelligent and flexible operation of whatever the enterprise does, from building ships to shipping potatoes to running a public agency.

Most VUZy by 1992 had involved a significant portion of their students in a three-way contract with an enterprise. In such a contract, the enterprise agrees to pay a fixed yearly sum to the VUZ for five years for preparation of a particular kind of specialist; the VUZ agrees to nurture and train such a specialist; and the student agrees to work for that particular enterprise, after graduation, for no less than a stipulated number of years—normally three to five years.

Amounts paid to the VUZy ranged from 25,000 rubles to 40,000 rubles per student per year as of fall 1992. Some of the students under such contract have already worked for their sponsoring enterprise before entering higher education.

Some technical institutes had (1992–93) such "three-way contracts" for up to 40 percent of their students, beginning with the students' first year of higher education. One dean expressed a hope that that percentage would increase, while another at a different VUZ hopes the proportion will *not* grow larger. The latter, an administrator in one of the Autonomous Republics of Siberia, does not favor allowing the central government to withdraw from its public responsibility for education. Ped. institutes, of course, occupy a different position, since local public schools have no funds for participating in such three-way contracts for their future teachers. Yet some ped. institutes report that enterprise do contract with them for certain types of specialists—for example, in English or another language that is in current demand by students with an eye on future careers in business.

By 1996, the number of such three-way contracts had declined abruptly, reflecting the many closed or failing enterprises in the region.

2. International sources.

In eastern Russia many VUZy have drawn up contracts to provide Asian governments with specified services. Most commonly, a VUZ accepts a contingent of students from China (PRC), instructs them in Russian language and culture and in some technical specialty for two years, meanwhile perhaps sending instructors to the Chinese institution for short periods. Sometimes, in these programs, the primary communication actually occurs in English, since neither party to the contract has sufficient expertise in the other's language! Korean graduate students and a few other East Asian students constitute further small sources.

At least one private American firm began, in 1994, providing North American students with an opportunity to study for one or more months in VUZy of Pacific Russia. With the written endorsement of a deputy minister of higher education, the Virtus Company of New York has arranged for its client students to study at the Khabarovsk State Technical University and at Tomsk State University, as part of a two-semester advanced study in Russian language and culture. From 1991–92, such arrangements did not require approval from beyond the VUZ.

There are various American university involvements, mentioned elsewhere, in collaborative instructional programs in business administration, management, market economics, western style accounting, and the like. Here we have set out only to list new types of income for VUZy which may continue to yield over the longer term. Yet the additional income earned by local faculty members from teaching in these programs—it can be argued—may significantly help them *and their departments* to ride out the current financial crises and thus have a direct effect on long-term survival of VUZy. At a minimum, eastern Russia has such American partner programs (F'96) at VUZy in Irkutsk, Khabarovsk, Vladivostok and Yakutsk.

3. Consulting.

In a few instances a VUZ, through one of its sub-units such as a department or faculty (sim. division), contracts with another entity to complete a research project or a service other than instructional ones for that entity. In a Khabarovsk VUZ, for example, a department head with approval of the dean competed for the opportunity to do studies, under contract, of stress on road bridges. The dean himself also collaborated with colleagues in a for-profit survey study of new personnel needs of employers in his region. While such consulting is commonplace to American faculty members, the "for profit" angle at least is new here. At present there appear to be few opportunities for it, and close estimation of the extent of faculty consulting is not feasible. As mentioned earlier, this source will likely grow again as local production and regional economy improve.

69

4. Physical facilities.

Most VUZy have physical facilities which they find it possible to rent to foreign or non-academic local organizations. The Far East State Maritime Academy has an excellent location astride the ridge of a peninsula and in easy walking distance from downtown Vladivostok. This Academy has a new indoor swimming pool, a large older auditorium, and a maritime historical museum, all available to the public on a fee basis. More commonly, VUZy rent space to a variety of concessionaires, from pizza to photocopying. (*See Chap. 4.*)

5. "Local" government.

A fifth possibility must be mentioned as a dynamic new source: the territory, republic or oblast' government. In at least the two republics in Pacific Russia, the republic's government has contributed to the support of higher education. While initially quite small, this is important politically and surely will grow along with the taxing capacity of such governments. They may well retain higher proportions of taxes collected, before remitting to Moscow. They already see higher educational institutions as part of the vital infrastructure on which to build their region's new economy.

Outlook for Non-Federal Support.

Of all five types of new sources listed above, the one with the greatest potential expansion within the decade could be #5, local/regional governments. Second to it stands #3, contract work by units of faculty members. It is impossible to estimate during this transitional moment the extent and economic significance of faculty "moonlighting" although decent survival just now drives all or most faculty members to seek additional sources of income. As organized units capable of doing contract research, however, some faculty structures have begun an activity comparable to the "grantsmanship" known in western universities.

As they look for appropriate research tasks, VUZy have begun to venture into a realm long the domain of research institutes under sponsorship of the Academy of Sciences. (Remember that VUZ stands for "higher *instructional* institution" and NII for "scientific *research* institute.") Meanwhile, federal support for those research institutes also has lagged seriously, forcing many academic professionals to do even more crossover work, mostly teaching, in nearby VUZy than normally has been the

70

case. Thus the current crisis could come to be seen, in retrospect, as the historical event which drew higher *instruction* and advanced *research* together into closer working relationships, structurally more similar to those within a western university.

In any case, the new circumstance of underfunding from the center brought VUZy and NII (research institutes) either into competition or into new forms of collaboration for the applied research tasks which regional economic entities need someone to perform. Until the large factories of the region go back to work, however, private entities will hardly have the resources needed to fund new research for their planning.

Thus recent shifts of authority, responsibility and financial support—all have worked together to link VUZy more closely with the economic needs of their own regions.

Policy Change (C.): End of Job Assignment/Guarantee System for Graduating Seniors.

By the beginning of the 1990s, as already noted, VUZy had ceased to observe the system of "assigned distribution" (*raspredelyenie*) of graduates—assignment of each new specialist to a particular job location. This had been an onerous practice. Top-ranked students had much choice in the matter, i.e. could state their preference among several positions and locations, but many good students found themselves sent to villages far from any familiar places or faces. New grads from teacher colleges in Siberia especially felt the brunt of society's need to staff rural schools, some with particular language needs for the remote area to which they were sent. They would serve a minimum of three years in that first job, some five, before they could be considered for a more desirable location.

Yet this military-like system of assignments carried its comforts, too. Obviously it eliminated the question of whether one's college education would lead to some kind of employment in one's field of preparation. With that, it enabled a modicum of continuity in family relationships. One could marry, look beyond the three-to-five-year contract toward a next position closer to the family network, either hers or his. To appreciate this system of assignments as a benefit, one need only to recall the many Americans with new B.A.s and B.S.s who find or create first jobs unrelated to the major they pursued with such enthusiasm a few months before. Some of the most curious restaurants and small shops in American cities—especially college towns—have arisen from the dashed hopes of recent history and English majors. So assignment to a first, diploma-related job could offer some comfort to American students as well. But suddenly at the dawn of the 1990's this system of manpower supply in Russian higher education was dropped.

When the job distribution system ended for most Russian graduating seniors, it sent a great shudder through entire student populations. It defined a moment whose practical effects will be debated by Russian professors and instructors into the future. Some will say that the "new" student since then is more diligent, more serious and focused. Others will point out students who became more self-centered, greedy—or alienated from their group, i.e. those with whom they entered their major. There is no apparent disagreement among instructors, however, that the end of the system of *raspredelyenie* marked a significant change in student attitudes toward their studies. It also changed the nature of relationships between the VUZy and regional employers, and the entire job marketplace.

Where they go.

What actually happens now to graduating seniors? Without *raspredelyenie,* there is no system for tracking them. Anecdotally it is known that many students while still students find part-time jobs in the style of their North American counterparts. Or they hang out with a group trying to start a new enterprise. An old American folk-saying claims that "Education creates jobs." It is here being put to a very stringent test. Recently, many try to leave the region until the economy improves. It is certain, however, that at present a large pool of young "specialists"—young adult Russians with a higher education—watches for the promised market economy to bloom. (More about "human resources" in Chapter 5.)

Mating season.

It seems fitting to mention, as addendum to this discussion of *raspredelyenie,* a cultural viewpoint in the Pacific end of Russia about the window of opportunity for marriage. Female students—even attractive ones—have lamented out loud that age 22 (graduation time) is the prime time for marrying. Miss that and it's all downhill from there. If a "girl" does not marry by her mid-twenties—so goes the tale locally—her chances for finding a *good* match abruptly diminish, if not disappear. Moral to the story? This cultural force continues to exert powerful pressure on students in Pacific Russia even while they outwardly appear as the most independent people in the country. It is striking that, side by side with financially tough times for faculty members, students today are among the very best-dressed people in town. Many a grandmother would sacrifice her porridge, if necessary, to see her grandchild complete the *diplom* in good style for whatever opportunity comes next. And for many, "opportunity" means more than job and income.

Quick Sketches of Higher Educational Institutions (VUZy) in Transition.

A brief close-up of several VUZy will help to put flesh on the bones of the discussion thus far. In particular, the following sketches illustrate several kinds of transition underway during the past decade, in higher education in Pacific Russia.

Birobidjan Pedagogical Institute, first higher educational institution to be established in the Jewish Autonomous Oblast', admitted its first students in 1990. The oblast' government helped to attract good staff members with free apartments in new housing. A leased building where most classes were meeting in 1992 appeared clean and bright, quality artworks were on exhibit in hallways. Stimulating displays of various subject matter, such as classroom teachers learn to assemble, filled classroom walls. Nearby, a new permanent building still under construction already housed some classes. The head of the International Affairs Office reported, in fluent New York English, that entering classes for each of the first three years have averaged somewhat more than 300; some students come from beyond the oblast', places like Yakutia (Sakha) and Magadan. This VUZ stands within a short walk of the center of town.

A small city with population of less than 60,000, Birobidjan sits astride the Trans-Siberian Railway within a two to three hour commute to Khabarovsk. It is the capital of the oblast' and has one of the best microclimates for agriculture in Pacific Russia. An important shoe factory stands at the opposite end of town from the Pedagogical Institute. After

1987 a hefty percentage of its population emigrated, ostensibly to Israel. By 1992 it was estimated that that wave of emigration had passed, and that the population will stabilize or grow. A handsome public hall for chamber music has just been completed. The town has an active sister city relationship with Beaverton, Oregon.

Fulfilling its original charge, Birobidjan Pedagogical Institute offers Yiddish language and Hebrew culture among its majors, together with a required English minor. Yiddish language, not Hebrew, is offered because this oblast' originally was to attract Jews from Eastern Europe, not to prepare them for emigration to Israel. In keeping with its border location, this Pedagogical Institute quickly added Chinese language to its curriculum. It also gives special place to environmental education, helping teachers to instill in their pupils an active and informed concern for their natural surroundings. One instructor told of leading classes on regular field trips to clean up a local tributary of the Amur River. Despite being landlocked several hundred miles inland from the Pacific, Birobidjan Ped. Institute has a formidable English Department with special emphasis on American English, in contrast with all-Soviet textbooks of British English.

The rector, a keen energetic man appointed from another Far East position to be midwife of this fledgling VUZ, notes that the oblast' has a primarily agricultural economy. Therefore he and his advisors have begun considering whether this Pedagogical Institute—the only VUZ in their oblast—ought to add a faculty of agronomy as a next adaptation to the local economy. (The rector complimented his visiting American researcher on their shared insight, that higher education serves as nerve center of any new economic system in the region.)

This new Pedagogical Institute, as teachers' colleges elsewhere, thus understands that it serves its host region as a general or multi-purpose college.

Buryat State University, long promised to the Republic of Buryatia, had its actual birth in 1991–92 as a *filial* (branch) of Novosibirsk State University. With a Buryat rector and prorector, it was on course with its opening class in September 1992 to develop quickly toward full university status. Its first anniversary celebration in '93 was attended by not only representatives of local government and enterprises, but even of China and, unofficially, California.

The Republic of Buryatia occupies a large territory on the east side of Lake Baikal and extends westward far past the southern end of the lake.

74

Outer Mongolia borders Buryatia on the south, and gives rise to the Selenga River, main tributary to Baikal. Since the 1600s Ulan Ude (oo-LAN-oo-DEH)—now with a population over 350,000—stands along the Selenga, and stands today the principal city and capital of Buryatia. Topographically, Buryatia resembles Colorado—plains, mountains, high fertile valleys. It has a strong Buddhist heritage, with spiritual ties directly to Tibet, and close cultural ties to Mongolia. Here, Genghis Khan is regarded as a local boy who made a significant difference in the world-at-large.

The new university rector (in '92–'93 officially called "director" of the *filial*) made clear his intention to draw on Buryat heritage to blend with western scientific and scholarly insights in working out unique approaches to the natural environment, sustainable use of resources, human health, and other fields. "This area is so rich in beauty and resources," the rector said earnestly, "we must not pass it on to our great-grandchildren as a wasteland, nor the population as a wasted people."

The rector quickly extended invitations to scholars in nations around the Pacific Rim, especially North America, for communication and collaborative efforts.

In 1995 this fledgling university was grafted onto the well-rooted trunk of **Buryat State Ped. Institute.** The teacher's college had a long history in Ulan Ude, an established library and other resources at its central location. It had an especially strong Department of English Language in a noted Faculty of Foreign Languages. Its rector also is Buryat, and a member of the republic's parliament. By itself this Ped. Institute was to receive university status. Now the new and the old institutions together constitute Buryat State University.

This newly combined Buryat State University is by no mans the only VUZ in town. A large and strong East Siberian State Technical Institute plus an Agricultural Institute and the East Siberian Institute of Culture also are located here. But the newly crafted university is clearly intended to serve as the flagship VUZ, with formative powers for the future economy of this Pacific-leaning republic.

Far East State Maritime Academy, Vladivostok, has a long history in that year-round port city. In 1991–92 it was upgraded from an *"uchilishche"* (specialized occupational school) to the full status of a VUZ. It now awards the five-year *diplom* for several kinds of specialization. It is one of only three maritime academies in the Russian Federation; a limited "higher college" (*uchilischche*) also operates at the port of Petropavlovsk–Kamchatka. So FESMA is the maritime academy for Russia's Pacific coast.

"FESMA" proudly relates that, in receiving this upgrade to academy/VUZ status, it also received instruction from the central ministry to serve an experimental function for the other maritime institutions. It bears special responsibility to try out new curricular approaches, new majors perhaps, or new processes for monitoring quality. It also proudly shows a visitor its state-of-the-art electronic equipment for training maritime navigators and pilots.

Vladivostok, a city with population over 600,000, is the home port of the Russian navy's Pacific Fleet, and is an all-year port (does not freeze shut). It is the Pacific terminus of the Trans Siberian Railway, the major landbridge for goods shipped between Europe and eastern Asia. The harbor has a complex structure of bays and inlets well protected from the open sea, topographically not unlike a San Francisco–Vallejo combination (i.e., north end, San Francisco Bay). In 1991 the city opened to foreign visitors, and by September 1992 the U.S.A. opened a new consulate in Vladivostok. Commercial activity, especially by sea and rail, quickly increased.

FESMA quickly added an office for international contacts, and by 1995 exchanged training ship visits with the California Maritime Academy, as well as calling at other Pacific ports previously off limits. In 1992 it already had high proficiency in its English language department. English, being the international language in international waters, is required for all majors leading to sea-going jobs. It offers majors also for land-based positions related to port management and equipment. The rector, during a 1992 interview, told of a first modest experiment with administering written final examinations in a science discipline.

In the first few years of the decade, FESMA had a high and growing percentage of its students supported in three-way contracts with shipping enterprises and other port-related employers. But by 1995–96 the widespread economic depression had reduced that severely, and an energy crisis had hit Vladivostok especially hard. Staff at FESMA reflected the general depression. Yet Vladivostok and neighboring Nakhodka remain the chief shipping and receiving doorway for Russia on the Pacific, so these ports and commercial freight carriers must grow eventually. FESMA awaits at the heart of that potentiality.

Vladivostok has, in addition to FESMA, at least eight other public institutions of higher education, including the Far Eastern State University and a large technical university. (It was not feasible to obtain a list of private/independent VUZy for this report.)

Khabarovsk State Technical University. The city of Khabarovsk (pop. 600,000), described at length in Chapter 1, has become Russia's Pacific point of entry for air traffic. Its newly-built international air terminal has expedited procedures for customs inspection and entry. Japan selected Khabarovsk for the location of its consulate on the Pacific. The Trans-Siberian Railroad passes through here, and the city's location on the Amur River makes it a nexus of river freight and trans-shipment activity. Paved highway connects it by auto with Vladivostok 500 miles to the south and Komsomol'sk-na-Amure 200 miles to the north. It has approximately fifteen VUZy, including ten public ones.

Until 1993 a polytechnical institute, Khabarovsk State Technical University has made swift changes aimed at making it a major regional university. Trimming back some traditional departments such as automotive engineering and the evening division, its new rector set up a center of computer science research, an office of international affairs at prorector level, a new school of liberal arts, an institute of information technologies, and an institute of economics and management. It teaches business law and environmental science insofar as they relate to its other technical specialties. While guiding such changes, the rector also chaired a regional advisory committee on the environment, and served a term in the (then new) federal duma! During these years, KhSTU's total enrollment fell, but it retained staff so as to attain an even richer student/faculty ratio of 7:1.

Promptly in 1991–92 a dean and several faculty members conducted a survey of employing entities—enterprises and local government units—in the territory, in order to estimate actual needs for engineers and other technically trained personnel in the nation's new economic situation. This initiative enhanced the VUZ's working relationships with a widespread set of enterprises in the Russian Far East. The university also has a major branch in the city of Magadan, now a depressed mining center 1,000 air miles to the north and capital of Magadan Oblast'.

In its new international outreach, KhSTU annually hosts a group of American students for the month of January (Russian language and area studies). It also contracts with a university in northern China to host a contingent of Chinese students on a two-year rotational program. They study Russian language and a technical field. KhSTU also has developed close relations with Korean institutions, while pursuing further inter-institutional opportunities widely around the Pacific basin.

In 1996–97 it published a 22-page, full-color brochure about itself in the English language. Since English serves as the international language in East Asia, this indicates a strong orientation to countries on both sides of the Pacific.

The foregoing sketches of selected institutions of higher education suggest in concrete detail how the VUZy of Pacific Russia use their new level of autonomy for adapting to economic and other needs of their own region. In considerable detail we have reviewed changes in authority, support, and programs of institutions of higher education in Pacific Russia. The next chapter discusses ways, both big and small, in which these VUZy are participating in the emerging, still-stringent regional economy.

Notes

1. V.G. Kinelev, chairman of Russia's Federal Committee for Higher Education, succinctly summarized the relevant section of the (new) Russian Constitution in his preface to: *Gosudarstvennyi obrazovatel'nyi standart vysshevo professional'novo obrazovaniya* (Federal Educational Standards for Professional Higher Education), Moscow, 1995 (pg. 3):

   Higher educational institutions have been freed from ideological and (governmental) administrative regulation and influencing; they have acquired actual autonomy, every opportunity now for complete realization of academic freedom—the freedom for teaching, freedom for research, and freedom for studying.

   Kinelev then proceeds to outline the delicate new task of setting national standards while not abrogating these new constitutional freedoms.
2. For month-by-month sampling of typical retail prices for food and household items, see monthly issues of the very informative *Russian Far East News,* Anchorage, University of Alaska, American Russian Center (first published 1992, discontinued 1997). Its September 1996 issue reported, for example, the following retail prices for early July '96 in Khabarovsk: 1 U.S. dollar = 5,100 rubles

1 U.S. dollar=5,100 rubles (July 1996)

Product	Cost (in rubles)
10 eggs	7,000
1 liter milk	3,600
1 loaf bread	2,800
1 kilo. apples	7,000
1 kilo. rice	5,500
1 liter gasoline	2,330
1 kilo. sugar	4,800
1 pack Marlboro cigarettes	6,000
1 liter Russian vodka	13,400
1 Snickers bar	2,700

4

Higher Education in the Economy of Pacific Russia
(First presented to AAASS Convention, 21 November 1993; revised 1998.)

During the Soviet era, the role of higher education in the Russian economy was discussed usually in terms of manpower planning. If attention turned to Siberia and the Far East, chronic turnover and shortage of trained manpower there were the common topics.[1] During Cold War decades, western scholars tended to adopt the Moscow view that, for the foreseeable future, the eastern regions of Siberia would remain dependent on European Russia to supply a large portion of their highly educated personnel. Even into the 1990s, however, the actual development of higher education in Pacific Russia and its *multiple roles* in the emerging economy there had yet to be examined.

This does not ignore the fact that, already in the Brezhnev era, historical reviews of several individual institutions appeared on a local basis (in Russian) as "jubilee anniversary" essays.[2] Also, useful survey studies of students—with all "Siberia" as one sub-group—were published after 1985 by the sociologist Zaslavskaya and colleagues.[3] One also could pick up case information from an occasional report published under the ministry in Moscow, where it might support targeted policy aims for education in Siberia or the Far East. Moreover, it long had been possible to glean bits of descriptive information on individual VUZy in Pacific Russia from an official Soviet publication, the annual "Handbook for Those Entering Higher Education Institutions in the USSR" (*Spravochnik dlya postupayuschchikh v vysshie uchebnye zavedeniya SSSR*), Moscow.

Nevertheless, higher education specifically in the eastern regions has not been analyzed for the ways it contributes to the regional economy during the current transitional decade. This dearth of analysis need surprise no one, for several reasons: (a) Changes, in higher education as in other sectors, have occurred at a very rapid pace during the past ten or twelve years. It is hard to capture this motion in published form. And, (b) Prior to the Yeltsin administration, the system was so standardized (each academic major had a nationwide serial number!) that a western scholar might plausibly generalize from the known VUZy in western Russia to the unknown VUZy of Siberia. (c) At the same time, following a Moscow habit, western scholars might have tended to discount the quality of institutions in "the provinces" farthest from the center, without studying them. This is not without its historical parallels in the U.S.

In Soviet times, manpower—"preparation of specialists"—was the sole contribution a Russian VUZ could expect to make to the economy, since organized research was kept separate from the teaching institutions. (One major exception to this was, ironically, in Siberia—the famous Akademgorodok model in Novosibirsk.) Even so, some writings on manpower in Siberia did not bother to distinguish between "highly educated" and "laborer" categories!

Aims and sources of this chapter.

The present chapter will sketch several different contributions by the VUZy of Pacific Russia to their regions' economic activity in the post-Gorbachev decade. It will illuminate ways by which recent changes in the VUZy, discussed in previous chapters, are affecting the economy. As Pacific Russia struggles to make the transitions work to improve life and lives, higher education becomes more tightly interwoven with the emerging regional economy. This discussion thus feeds into a continuing theme of the book: that Pacific Russia can now be "courted for its mind," its human resources, and not only for its raw, natural resources.

Information used here includes firsthand findings from extensive research journeys by the author to seven cities and more than twenty institutions on the Pacific end of the Russian Federation, 1986 through 1996.[4] A dozen were visited two or more times.

I. Background.

Diversifying by Region.

As mentioned in previous chapters, various changes have led to *greater individuation among VUZy.* In the 1990s, not only has Russian higher education changed but individual VUZy in Pacific Russia have changed in directions they themselves deemed appropriate to regional or local needs. At least in the eastern regions, they have drawn closer to employers, local government agencies, and even partner organizations in neighboring Pacific countries. Nearly all VUZy have initiated some kinds of efforts to adjust to new economic realities which they face, including direct foreign relationships.

Going global.

During this same time, of course, other Pacific Rim countries also have been undergoing rapid economic changes, especially ones imposed by technological change and the emerging so-called "global marketplace." Furthermore, local industries which, in Soviet times, dominated and fed a particular urban center do not necessarily continue their relevance since the passing of the command economy. For example, a small city once dependent on producing shoes for wide distribution in the Soviet Union now has to face (a) much higher transportation and marketing costs to get to their customary markets, (b) increasing shoe imports from neighboring China, and (c) the competing range of styles from a global bazaar and a regional free trade zone! In the face of such complex change in such a short time, VUZy have some new missions. Obviously, many individuals within VUZy also have to make new adjustments. Against such a background, VUZy are playing multiple roles in the regional economy.

II. Supply of "specialists" (VUZ graduates) within the region.

To begin with the manpower supply question: Do the eastern VUZy now supply their own regions' needs for highly educated and trained persons? In general terms, there are two answers: (a) Yes, since there is now an oversupply for industries that still function and employ college graduates: and (b) Who knows?—since conditions now require people for emerging enterprises and for creating new employment. (*See "Renovating Curricula" below.*)

Intake/Admissions.

In a high proportion of institutions, the size of entering classes was reduced after 1987—at least the numbers approved and supported by the central government ministries. These reductions occurred in technical institutes and universities rather than in teachers' colleges. More than one prorector, in reporting raw figures, carefully explained that these reductions had occurred as a result of local and more accurate estimates of the future needs of the enterprises, not from lack of applicants. Later, the support figures changed again, and VUZy began to recruit new students who could pay their own tuition and additional "fees" for admission. Institutional survival triumphed over formerly fixed admission quotas.

In the Soviet past, some say, the enterprises employing college graduates grandly inflated their needs for additional, highly-trained persons. In this they resembled American aerospace firms during some decades, "stockpiling" engineers and mathematicians in expectation of the next military contract on a cost-overrun basis. In the 1990s the VUZy at last gained the power to correct such overestimating while holding constant the number of teaching staff. Among higher education institutions, this reduced intake of first-year students occurred at approximately the same time everywhere. One result was, of course, a further enriched student/faculty ratio—fewer students per instructor. This ratio had already been better than on most American campuses. *(See Table 9, p. 97)*

Another result of smaller student enrollment (still talking about number of student places supported by government, i.e. "FTE" (Full-Time Equivalent) students in U.S. administrative jargon) was increased competition among applicants. In some faculties it ranged as high as five applicants per space. Rectors of several VUZy reported with visible pleasure that the early '90s thus brought them additional powers for improving the quality of student ranks. They also assumed the right to discharge students who perform poorly, rather than allowing them to pass along through several years with unacceptable grades.

Meanwhile, a small number of faculties began to try using *written* examinations. Whatever else its merits may be, this practice reduces the chances of favoritism and bribery. Those occur more easily when exams are brief oral recitations before a panel of two or three underpaid instructors. At the same time, however, more "non-budgeted" students were being admitted on the basis of private payments—the "Chechnya effect," military conscription.

New graduates, annual (estimate).

With the help of such changes as described above, overall attrition (drop-out) rates remain low in comparison with U.S. public colleges and universities. On average, from a VUZ's total fall enrollment (i.e. five-year complement of undergraduate students), between 10 percent and 18 percent graduate in the following year. A 20 percent graduation would mean, of course, no attrition at all, if annual admission rates remained constant over five years. (*See Table 8 for sample of 10 VUZy and graduation totals.*)

Using the foregoing range of graduation rates from VUZy of Pacific Russia, one can estimate that *upwards of 16,500 new college/university graduates* emerge each year, looking for meaningful, full-time employment in the new economy of their region. (*See Appendix A.*)

Destinations.

Inquiries at several VUZy indicate that new graduates, into the mid-1990s, generally remain in Pacific Russia. From here they show little desire to migrate to Moscow unless financial stress ultimately makes that necessary. Any assumption that the ablest youth from Pacific-leaning regions still—as in Soviet times—naturally aspire to make a career leap to Moscow, must be supported with adequate data. We have not found it to be so, except in financial despair. It must be acknowledged that, by 1994–95, financial stress caused a 1 percent net emigration from the Far East, much of it reportedly to western Russia. *Of those who left, the portion of those over age 16 who had completed some higher education was over 30 percent.*[5] But anecdotal evidence suggests that such people went to relatives—in whatever city—who could help them find work. One contention in this book is that living conditions in several urban centers of Pacific Russia have become such that second- and third-generation inhabitants choose to remain here if financial conditions permit. Or to return here when they can.

Of course young adults want to venture forth, to "seek their fortune" in places that attract them, stimulate them, hold promise of prosperity. The net out-migration (above) first became noticeable in 1995. For young people of Pacific Russia, however, the work desired was more likely to be in Anchorage, Seattle, Tokyo or Sydney than in western Russia. In fall 1996 one American visitor had requests for help in getting U.S. work visas from four educated families whom he'd known 4 years. No requests before that time. For them, "To come back home" meant "return to the *Pacific* end of Russia." (*See Chapter V, "employability."*)

III. Helping to Define a Regional Economy.

What kind of economic situation awaits the new graduates and others hoping to use their higher education here? Volumes continue to be published about economic conditions in Russia, and special newsletters focus on this theme for Pacific Russia. This chapter therefore will not attempt a detailed or complex discussion of the theme, but simply call attention to a few salient factors with an immediate relation to higher education.

Growth of private employment.

In 1996 the U.S. Embassy in Moscow issued the following statement regarding the Russian Federation.

Contrary to the view of many in Russia and the West, Russia's growing business class is neither predominantly corrupt nor overwhelmingly wealthy. It is composed of self-employed entrepreneurs and also includes well-paid professionals working for foreign and large Russian companies. This upwardly-mobile group is considerably more inclusive than indicated by the term *New Russians,* which has become muddled with over- and misuse. . . . While far from representing a majority of Russians, this group is considerably larger than generally understood in the West. . . .

The emerging business class . . . is relatively young . . . below 40 and many of the brightest stars are under 35. . . . Backgrounds tend to be technical (math., science, engineering) . . . neither flashy nor flush. This nascent commercial middle class has formed and become upwardly mobile because it offers needed skills and . . . (is) among the first Russians to find niches in the post-Soviet economy.

> —U.S. Embassy, Moscow
> (in *Russian Far East News,* 6/1996, Alaska Ctr. for International Business, University of Alaska, Anchorage, Alaska 99508)

This report seemed, in 1996, to represent the situation in at least three cities of Pacific Russia. As shown in the walk along main street Khabarovsk (Chap. 1), there is not only persistent public effort to rebuild civic infrastructure, but also substantial private energy and individual investment in new, mostly small enterprise. If the American record of small business failure can serve as a guide, most of these efforts will fail. No claim is made here that business in Pacific Russia has less travail than in the U.S.! Yet this overall investment of talent, energy and private resources represent the "cambium layer," the local potential for growth. And most of it stands upon a foundation of new higher education.

Interaction with VUZy.

In fact, many in this new entrepreneurial class are also—at the same time—engaged in higher education. Some are students, some instructors. These are not only clerks, watchmen, and cosmetics firm representatives; they also include partners in small businesses, computer operators, and individual tradesmen. More than one professor joked wrily to colleagues in 1995–96, "A couple of my (current) students are already making more money than I am."

Some individuals plunge into business and then, with practical problems they do not know how to solve, seek help in a nearby VUZ. A chain of centers for applied business training, managed by the University of Alaska, are located in VUZy facilities and hosted by VUZy. At these academic centers, visiting American business practitioners and consultants not only offer applied classes and short-series workshops for local Russian entrepreneurs, but also counseling about problems in the specific businesses of local clients. Thus they do not compete with longer courses and major programs in Management, Business and Economics offered by the

VUZ, but operate like an extension program supplementing them. VUZy have long operated teaching institutes for "raising the qualifications" of working professionals. But for second careers in private business—that's something else! This is but one example of direct interaction between VUZy and the new entrepreneurs of Pacific Russia.

Renovating infrastructure.

Delay and underpayment of wage obligations by the federal (Moscow) government, high and rising prices, irrational layers of taxes, falling production in major industrial sectors—these dismal facts of economic life in Pacific Russia have been widely reported and published. One huge area of economic need, meanwhile, does show signs of improvement: renovating and modernizing infrastructure. Chapter 1, in an illustrative walk along "Main Street," pointed to common civic improvements, such as public buildings, city streets, and water supply systems. Other renewal projects, however, take on more regional or even national significance, such as those in transportation systems and communications.

A project to improve the Trans-Siberian Railway system, for example, has importance for big oil projects on Sakhalin Island, the ports of Vladivostok, Nakhodka, and Vanino, perhaps even for the new Svobodnyi cosmodrome (the next "Baikonur") in Amur Oblast'. Already one of the top railroads of the world, the Trans-Siberian was made even more prominent by the 1967 Suez crisis as one of the key landbridges on Earth. The TSRR mainline has been fully electrified for years, but electronic communication systems are said to be part of its present makeover.

Viewed against this TSRR background (to say nothing about the saga of the "star-crossed" BAM, a 1990s northerly route to Pacific waters), it is useful to notice changes in one institution of higher technical education. Recent adaptations in the nature and name of the Khabarovsk Railway Engineering Institute suggest its close involvement in the economy of its region.

In 1994–95 this railway engineering institute became the "Far East Academy of Communication Ways" (a literal translation of . . . *Akademiya putei soobshcheniya.* For local continuity it is actually called "Far Eastern State Transport Academy.") In a 1996 interview, a vice president underscored the intent of this name change: to cover more "ways" than rail transport, and especially to embrace electronic communication.

In restructuring this institute, they established a School of Management, Automation and Telecommunications. Among other majors here, they included: (1) automation and control systems, (2) telemechanics, (3) microprocessor information control, (4) circuits and types of data transmission. There is a Department of Electro-energetics—energy supply, a critical current problem in southeastern Russia. They established an Institute of Economics and Management. The School for International Students has a special major in International Economic Relations (two- and four-year programs). From an entering class of 1,578 students in fall, '92, these changes helped to attract an entering class of 2,107 in fall '94 (33 percent leap).

This VUZ continues its close relations with the railroad industry. Yet its reorganization clearly indicates that it plans an active role, as well, in the larger fields of transportation, energy, and communications—all vital segments of the regional economy.

In another regional VUZ, Khabarovsk Technical University, swift changes reveal its determination to stay "ahead of the curve" in the economic remaking of its region. From 1992 through 1995 it added the following majors to its total offerings:

Finance and Credit	Mathem'l. Methods & Economic Research
Commerce	Business Law
Social Work	Renovation of Machine-Building
Info. Systems in Machine-Building	Info. Systems in City and State Management
Standardizing & Certifying in Machine-Building	Land Use Planning

In the Russian Far East machine-building, despite handicaps, accounted for the largest share ($ value) of exports in 1996. In fact a further look at this list, with one eye on the current status of the region's economic transition, indicates that this VUZ has made bold commitments to its territory's (i.e. *krai*) economic development.

School teaching and the economy.

Fear of unemployment after college had, already in 1993, a basis in fact. One dean at a technological institute in Buryatia reported, for example, that because of plant shrinkage and closures in that region, 80 to 90 percent of her graduates in 1993 had not found jobs by September 1.

Newer students, in choosing a major, have not remained oblivious to the new conditions of the local/regional economy. They have shifted their preferences from some academic fields to others, according to what they believe holds future promise for their careers. It resembles shifts of preference that occurred in Africa's new nations as they shed colonial status in the 1960's; young African students began to select academic majors in keeping with the way they perceived their new opportunities and responsibilities in administering a country. In Pacific Russia, students now flock to schools of business, management, economics, computer science/electrical engineering, English and Asian languages, *and school teaching.*

It is interesting to notice the first effect of the economic transition (and uncertainties) on teacher preparation institutions ("Pedagogical Institutes"). The following sample of 10 VUZy—East Siberia and Far East—includes four Pedagogical Institutes (Table 8). They reported their total fall enrollments for 1987 and for either 1992 or '93, plus total graduates in '92–'93 academic year.

One fact stands out immediately: In that five-year period of great national uncertainty, enrollment in the Pedagogical Institutes grew substantially, while others fell or remained the same.

Table 8: Total Enrollment and Graduating Seniors from Ten Higher Education Institutions, Eastern Siberia and Russian Far East, 1987–1992-93.

Name of Institution	Enrollment 1987	1992	1993	Completed "Diplom" 1992–93
Buryat Pedagogical Institute	2,437	4,100		652
Chita Pedagogical Institute	3,643	3,687		607
Chita Polytechnical Institute	4,040	3,298		571
Far East Commercial Institute	2,000	1,900		350
Irkutsk Inst. Of Economy	7,631		6,077	650
Irkutsk Pedagogical Institute	3,189	3,425		605
Irkutsk Polytechnical Institute	19,608	12,320		2,480
Irkutsk State University	8,317		7,326	1,044
Khabarovsk Pedagogical Institute	2,897		3,370	624
Khabarovsk Technical University	11,500	8,000		860
TOTALS	65,262	[53,503]		8,443

(Data reported to author by individual institutions. Dale M. Heckman, 11/93)

89

School teachers, at first glance not directly affecting the economy, have an important role in the long-discussed task of "stabilizing a resident population" in areas of Siberia. Teachers generally are in short supply. City schools have two shifts of pupils per day, six days per week.

Obviously, in such a period of employment uncertainty, the assurance that schools will continue to need qualified teachers adds to the attractiveness of Pedagogical Institutes. So the pedagogical institutes increased enrollments, while experiencing the present economic pressures in terms of students' changed preferences for "majors"; some students now chose different majors from 8 or 9 years ago.

As mentioned earlier, instruction in American-English has become a growth industry in VUZy of Pacific Russia. English language is seen as a route to employment in new international enterprises; it is used not only for commerce with North American interests but also as the common language with Chinese, Japanese and Koreans. Administrators in the Ped. Institutes realize that their institutions are preparing not only school teachers but professionals for a variety of other kinds of positions. Students realize, meanwhile, that an office secretary able to translate Russian into English probably can earn more money than an English teacher in a secondary school. So increased enrollments of English majors do not promise increased numbers of school teachers.

Alumni into the legislature.

One additional connection between ped. institutes and the regional economy stems from the fact that a significant number of elected representatives ("deputies") to regional (krai, oblast', and federal) parliaments have graduated from ped. institutes. If a new graduate goes to teach school in a village or remote town, he or she finds high expectations bestowed by local citizens—the teacher becomes part of the local *intelligentsia.* Then, to be elected to the duma seems neither surprising nor a long shot. And the duma determines tax rates. Also, more than one VUZ rector has held high political office while still a rector.

Village schools.

Do villages receive enough teachers to maintain their schools, encourage stability in their own population? This study has no overall statistical answer for that important question, but some indicative findings.

On a visit to the village of Gvasnyugi, heart of the indigenous Udege people, Khabarovsk krai, the author had an informal conversation with two schoolteachers at the end of a weekday (fall '93)—an Udege kindergarten teacher and a Russian math teacher for the secondary level. Both concurred that their school had its full complement of teachers except for a physical education instructor, that their classes enjoyed a good teacher-to-pupil ratio, but that the surrounding population had shrunk in recent years. Teachers at their school had received their training from several regional teachers colleges, not all from the nearest one. The conversation ended politely but abruptly as the village store opened (approx. 3:30 P.M.) and the new bread supply became available.

In the Buryat Republic (Eastern Siberia), staff of the teachers college in Ulan Ude said that Buryat people have tended to return from other parts of the USSR and of the Russian Federation, and that new teachers want to find teaching jobs among their "own people." This includes, for some, locating in villages outside and beyond the principal cities. Usually such duty entails the necessity to carry water and use outdoor plumbing, yet on the other hand, the teacher does not pay for electricity and some other services.

If one has some family network nearby, that is a great advantage, and the natural environment here is superb. In any case the teaching staff at the Ped. Institute, while aware of chronic shortages, did not feel that the rural schools of Buryatia have a vacancy crisis.

Of the graduating class of 1993 from the Ped. Institute in Buryatia, as of September, a quick check on those known to have obtained teaching positions, by location of the position, yielding the following:

Those graduates now teaching schools in Ulan Ude, the republic's capital and the main urban center of Buryatia: 96. Those teaching schools in towns and villages: 105. These data tend to confirm the opinions of instructors at the Pedagogical Institute, at least with regard to Buryatia. Many new teachers are trying village life.

The military factor.
The supply of school teachers has depended also on the size of military garrisons—important economic "sector." Military wives, according to common report by educators, traditionally follow where their husbands are assigned and accept the given local conditions as the price of a second family income. Such "captive" teachers continue to fill a substantial number of teaching positions in southern and eastern Siberia and the Rus-

sian Far East—i.e. the populated border areas. The more officers, evidently, the larger the supply of potential school teachers.

Import more manpower?

It would be foolhardy to generalize during this historic transition period that Pacific Russia—from Irkutsk Oblast' to the Pacific—has all the skilled manpower that it needs. *Who can accurately estimate its needs?* Yet no one in these regions today calls for "intellectual reinforcements" or skilled management help from western Russia. What they want from Moscow is back wages and a larger share of their tax payments to be returned for their own region's economic development. One hears this sentiment echoed around the dinner table by ethnic Russians as well as others: "But we'll provide our own managers."

There indeed remains a shortage of unskilled and low-skilled labor. First-year VUZ students and even school children, in September–October 1993 still went by the busload to help with the harvest on nearby farms. Brigades of Chinese laborers come under contract to forests, farms, and large projects. Soldiers work on civilian construction. But for professional levels of work, there is no evident lack of college graduates.

In terms of college-level preparation Siberians and Far Easterners generally concur that they need no supplementary specialists from "outside for work based in metropolitan areas." There already are too many college graduates working as shopclerks. The predominant evidence suggests that the VUZy of Pacific Russia provide an adequate supply of educated manpower for filling even the normal needs in urban areas. The problem with such a statement, of course, is determining what "normal" will mean when some former industrial enterprises get reorganized for work! One clear need now is sustained interaction with other Pacific Rim countries, appropriate colleagues with whom to engage in collaborative work. Meanwhile on an anecdotal level, several of the ablest young graduates in our acquaintance have become representatives in their region for North American companies. The current process of finding or creating employment for new grads seems no more orderly in Pacific Russia than it is in California!

Several programs have enabled small numbers of high school pupils and postsecondary students to spend one or two semesters in the United States. Not only the classroom experience but also the in-depth cultural exposure contributes to—among other things—their firsthand understanding of America's consumer economy.

At the university level, some visiting students (to the U.S.) concentrate on studying aspects of applied economics, and even receive a summer apprenticeship before returning to their home institution. The (U.S. Sen.) Bradley Program, administered by the American College Teachers of Russian (ACTR), supports several score of such youth from Pacific Russia each year. In 1996 the ACTR field office in Vladivostok created a résumé bank of Russian participants—alumni—in the Bradley year in the U.S. This bank serves as a free resource for enterprises (commercial and otherwise) to locate fluent English-speaking prospects for employment.

Summary of "educated manpower."

Thus, the "manpower supply"/human resources question now has become a matter of higher education's helping to define the question itself. That is, as factories and other enterprises have closed in Pacific Russia, and as new ones open, the whole understanding of an "economy" continues to evolve. "Market economy" yes but, combined with political changes, what kinds of educated people does that require for this region? In what proportions? Rather than continue to train X number of personnel for the requisitioned X number of job slots, in this pivotal decade the higher educational institutions (VUZy) are helping to shape the people who help to *create* the new employment needs in their own region! Through modest shifts in the profile of the typical student, through bold changes in the curricula offered, and through direct international exposure on their Pacific end of Russia, the VUZy have taken initiatives to re-define human resources for the emerging economy of Pacific Russia.

IV. Direct Ventures in Enterprise.

Driven mostly by an instinct for survival, institutions of higher education have found further ways of "engaging the economy" of the region. While each way by itself may seem negligible, together they appear much more significant in their local economic effect.

As host.

Most VUZy by now rent space inside their buildings to tradespeople to sell designated goods. In the main "corpus" of a university, separate small, private shops sell photocopy services, writing/drawing supplies, audiocassettes, newspapers, books, snacks, cosmetics, toiletries, and clothing items. Occasionally, trade is freestyle. In one VUZy an inquirer, following up on a newspaper advertisement, walks searchingly down a long, dimly-lit corridor and into a dean's outer office. There he apologetically asks the lone secretary about the ad. Without further word she brings out from her closet four rolls of the bargain-priced toilet paper, which she herself has advertised! But it is rented shops, plus the purveyors of lunchtime baked goods, that appear prominently as regular retail enterprises.

As venturer.

In several ways, VUZy now also operate their own small businesses for profit. The computer science institute of one university has architectural drawings and other advanced plans for a new "Visiting Scholars Center"—a hotel and conference center where they can host (for profit) scholarly conferences of interregional and international scope. In another city, a VUZ near the financial and transportation hub has found that it can open its new indoor swimming pool on a commercial basis, as well as a renovated auditorium. The international office of yet a third VUZ works with staff of its "international hostel" (dormitory) to make sure that that resource continues to show a profit.

At least one major technical institute has established an office of a special vice president (*prorector*) for commercial ventures (not actual title). This office has a parallel, of course, in what U.S. colleges/universities call the vice president for "development." But in the Russian case, this V.P. must concern himself mostly with profitable new enterprises for his institution rather than with wealthy alumni, foundations and corporations. In the particular case interviewed, the administrator outlined how he had set up an entity very much like a university foundation. Legally separate from the VUZ, this foundation can operate certain enterprises on a commercial, for-profit basis, and contribute its profits annually to the VUZ. It also transmutes commodity gifts—e.g. construction materials—into cash, like a frontier American preacher having received two barrels of pickles as an offering.

As community resource.

Not at all new in principle, a "board of community advisors" to a VUZ now serves a slightly different function than in Soviet times. At least a few rectors have gathered together an advisory group consisting of prominent business and political persons in their cities. Such a group has no official authority over the VUZ but receives visibility for its meetings and sage advice to the VUZ. What the rector of the institution receives in return, however, is (a) the favorable attention of these "elite" advisors, and (b) their implied obligation to find additional sources of support for the VUZ from their sectors, both private and governmental. This practice has been useful to colleges and universities in the U.S., and it marks a new stage of evolution for Russian VUZy and their growing mutual relations with local and regional entrepreneurs.

As one variant, in Khabarovsk 1992 a coalition of tech. university, business and local government persons marshalled financial support for a new elite high school to prepare bright kids in using computers and American-English language. The first class to graduate from that high school (1994) reportedly won very high marks in their first year in the local VUZ. At least one student swiftly made her way to a degree in a California university. What is especially notable here is the quick collaboration of a university with local commercial interests to "train up" a kind of student they all believe is needed.

Thus, not only as the suppliers of trained manpower but also as hosts to small business, as sponsors of their own enterprises, and as essential players in redefining the region's manpower needs—in all these ways the institutions of higher education affect and participate in the emerging new economy of Pacific Russia.

V. Academic Manpower.

A crucial question which usually remains quite obscure in discussing "the economy" anywhere is, how to replace the teachers of the expert leaders for that economy. When the professors leave and/or retire, whence come their qualified successors? Maintaining the quality of scholarship poses an acknowledged problem during this period of special financial stress. Just as at leading California universities recently, East Russian VUZy now have difficulty retaining their most noted scholars and attracting the best new ones.

Although "academic manpower" constitutes only part of the intelligentsia, Frederick Starr has forecast about the Russian intelligentsia:

Nor will members of the intelligentsia preserve their old support from the state. This will force them to become more truly independent. . . . (and they will) engage in new forms of activity.[6]

The professoriate—at least those on the lower half of the pay scale—has indeed lost some of its old support from the state and, according to many, some of the public's high regard as well. The sheer financial need for faculty members to find second and third jobs, many of them completely outside of academia, has been discussed earlier. Some have left to teach in foreign universities. Do the VUZy, including universities, of eastern Russia have the capability of ensuring their own survival by preparing young scholars and replenishing their own faculty ranks?

The rector of Khabarovsk State Technical University—a large polytechnical institute upgraded to a university—firmly says "Yes!" to that question. Authority and responsibility for examining applicants for the scholarly degree *Kandidat nauk* long resided exclusively in Moscow or western Russian circles. (*Kandidat* is most comparable to a doctorate, whether academic—Ph.D.—or professional in the U.S.) But now this regional technical university has the right to perform that function in many specialties. This rector—a scientific scholar in his own right—believes that in five years his institution will be preparing scholars at the *kandidat* level for most technical fields in the large Khabarovsk territory. Leaders of other universities in Pacific Russia also report receiving such authority, specialty by specialty. This marks a major shift in Russia's academia. It is like, in the tool-making industry, receiving a set of dies (molds) for making the tool-making machinery, instead of depending on a single source for that machinery.

Leap in Graduate Students.

Judging by the increased number of applicants for *Kandidat* degree studies, the judgment of these rectors is accurate. (A North American reader must understand that graduate student places have been far fewer, proportionately, in Russian institutions than in the U.S. There still are comparatively few T.A.s—teaching-assistant fellowships, *assistenty,* for instance.) Most VUZy that had any places in 1987 for *"aspiranty"* (graduate students) recently increased their number by large percentage jumps. The Irkutsk Institute of Economics, for example, increased the number of *aspiranty* places from 18 to 35, the Irkutsk State University from 94 to 127, and the Pedagogical Institute (*now* university) of Khabarovsk managed to increase from 8 to 34.

So not all change has been negative for instructional staffs. As the size of some entering classes was cut, the number of faculty positions was *not* cut in proportion. The "student/faculty ratio" grew richer (*See Table 9*). This looms all the more significant when one realizes that these institutions generally do not employ *aspiranty* for lecturing.

Table 9: Enrichment of Student/Faculty Ratio at Selected Institutions of Higher Education, Pacific Russia, 1987 to 1992–93.

Institution (VUZ)	Student/Instructor Ratio	
	1987	1992–93
Chita Pedagogical Institute	9.9/1	8.7/1
Chita Polytechnic Institute	11.5/1	8.5/1
Far East Commercial Institute	8.9/1	7.1/1
Irkutsk Inst. Of Economy	13/1	9/1
Irkutsk State University	10.5/1	8/1
Khabarovsk Technologicl Univesity	11/1	7/1

(Data in table as reported by individual VUZy to author, 1992–93.)

In any case, academic authorities in the Center have bestowed a critical right on their colleagues (and former students) in Pacific Russia. Just as the Soviet (now Russian) Academy of Sciences earlier recognized an official Branch Academy for Siberia and then a Branch for the Far East, so now the educational authorities grant to certain faculties in Pacific Russia the right to examine applicants for scholarly degrees. Graduate students still have the right to ask some noted authority in Moscow, St. Petersburg or elsewhere to serve on the degree advising/examining committee. But in most fields and specialties, evidently, the center has acknowledged the east's sufficient expertise for re-filling its own ranks.

It is too early to conclude that sufficient high-quality young scholars are stepping forth to fill those ranks. In North America, tough economic times tend to drive up enrollments in graduate schools. A similar effect may be happening in Pacific Russia. Yet that does not automatically mean that the best will remain and teach. In a recent decade, California's public universities found it so hard to attract good engineers into teaching engineering that they (institutions) sought permission to pay a higher scale for that one field. Doubtless, newly-crowned *Kandidaty* in some fields will find more lucrative employment in industries other than higher education. But their preparation and examination can occur now at a Pacific Russian

VUZ. Meanwhile, instructors continue to meet their classes with surprising tenacity.

VI. Environmental Studies and the Economy.

In a previous chapter it was mentioned that Environmental Studies has swiftly become part of curricula in Pacific Russian VUZy. In the schools, too, there now is some level of instruction about caring for the natural environment. To future elementary teachers, waste-water treatment specialists and air conditioning specialists, ecological concerns are being introduced. Not that this theme is new to the public! Three decades ago, public outcry arose on behalf of Lake Baikal and against industrial pollution there.[7] but now it has entered VUZ curricula. Yakutsk U., for example, has a *Kafedra* (Chair) of Ecology, and a major in it. Elsewhere, a professor of environmental science cautions against optimism, pointing to lack of enforcement of environmental laws. Still, the theme now has a regular place in university classes.

Here it bears pointing out that heightened environmental interest reflects also a certain *economic* attitude. For, here in the eastern provinces, from Lake Baikal to the Kamchatka fisheries, environmental stewardship blends directly into a regional sentiment, "Let's take care of *our own resources.*" It distinguishes between local control and control by others. The new regional environmentalism keeps alive a recent lesson, "Remember Hyundai!"—the Korean corporation that allegedly overcut Russian timber even beyond its contract. Thus to the extent it represents a green movement, environmental studies prepares an informed public if the central government deals away regional resources without adequate regional participation or control. It reinforces local feelings that "these resources are ours to care and plan for" because the region has become permanent home.

Moving On

The foregoing findings indicate an important economic re-focusing by higher education in Pacific Russia. Forced by a decline in financial support from central government, leaders of the institutions are finding ways to say "We'll do it ourselves." It is dreadfully hard simply to hold a VUZ together financially. But supporting and using higher education has become, in one decade, more a matter of local and regional concern. Although still answerable to federal authority, a university or institute in the east now feels more like a resource for its own region's economy and less a tool of some central long-range plan. Krai and republic governments have, as yet, little taxing power compared to the federal government, so their support for most VUZy probably remains token. Yet some VUZ leaders have worked proactively to anticipate or even lead the kinds of changes needed for an emerging regional economy. The strong sentiment among Pacific Russians for managing their own economic resources includes a clear resolve by VUZy—as one type of economic resource—to play a formative role in the transition.

Notes

1. (pg. 80) See, for example, discussions by J. Hardt and by V. Conolly in R. Swearingen (ed.): *Siberia and the Soviet Far East;* Hoover Institution Press, 1987.
2. (pg. 80) Example: *Irkutskii gosudarstvennyi universitet—krupneishii uchebno-metodicheskii i nauchnyi tsentr Vostochnoi Sibiri—kratkii istoricheskii ocherk* (Irkutsk Federal University—Major Instructional and Scientific Center of Eastern Siberia; a brief historical sketch); Irkutsk, 1978.
3. (pg. 80) Zaslavskaya and colleagues surveyed students and instructors of Siberia, in the late 1980s, for their opinions about *perestroika* as well as about personal habits and mores.
4. (pg. 81) List of VUZy visited at least once for present research project: Table 10, below.
5. (pg. 84) See esp. pp. 135ff. in OECD Report: Labour Dynamics in the Russian Federation.
6. (pg. 95) In *NewsNet* of the American Assoc. of Advancement of Slavic Studies (AAASS).
7. (pg. 98) For an early narrative account of "green" movement origins at Baikal, see Farley Mowat: *The Siberians.*

Table 10: Institutions of Higher Education in East Siberia and Russian Far East Visited by Author, 1986–96 for the Present Study

Birobidjan Pedagogical Institute**

Buryat Pedagogical University*

Buryat State University**

Chita Pedagogical Institute

Chita Polytechnical Institute

East Siberian Polytechnic Institute

Far East Commercial Institute

Far East State Maritime Academy*

Far East State University

Far East Technological Institute

Far East Academy of Public Admin.**

Far East Academy of Transport & Communication*

Irkutsk Institute of National Economy

Irkutsk Pedagogical Institute

Irkutsk Pedagogical Institute of Foreign Languages*

Irkutsk Polytechnic Institute

Irkutsk State University

Khabarovsk Inst. Of Management**

Khabarovsk Inst. Of National Economy

Khabarovsk Pedagogical University*

Khabarovsk State Technological University*

Russo-Asian University of Liberal Arts**

Yakutsk State University

Key: *means the status of this institution has been raised since 1987, e.g. from polytechnical institute to university.
         **means the institution itself has been established since 1987.

100

5

Pacific Russia's Readiest Resource
(A Generation of University Graduates Waits)

What kind of profile does a typical college graduate offer, in Pacific Russia? That is, what state of professional readiness does he/she bring to a job with a collaborative enterprise? The answer to this general question bears obvious importance for the success and durability of a business venture into this region. Firms from abroad will want to raise the question prior to unpacking their suitcases here.

As a way to tap concrete aspects of this human resources question, one can ask, "Once hired, what is the Russian college graduate *still likely to need* for working well in a Russian-American firm or project?" In fact this question was asked in interviews with both Americans and Russians involved in employment of college/university graduates in Pacific Russia. How did they respond? The following paragraphs illustrate the findings.

Russian Responses.

(1) On-site mentor. Katya (not her actual name) has excellent American-English language proficiency, a gentle manner and a good sense of humor. A college graduate and not yet thirty, she seems to fit well and comfortably as receptionist and administrative assistant in a Russian-American project housed in uptown Khabarovsk. The office maintains a busy daily schedule and functions in an informal "American west" style—small meetings, either scheduled or spontaneous, convene at a central table near the samovar, while other office functions continue around them. Hot drinks are always available. Visitors charge through the main door at any time. Managers do not noticeably keep track of short absences by staff. In this atmosphere Katya functions with aplomb, shifting easily between English and Russian, between visiting consultants, telephone and strangers. Although her bosses are bilingual, Katya can interpret for visitors as needed.

In a quiet moment Katya is asked, "In your experience what does it take for a new Russian graduate to succeed in a collaborative enterprise with Americans?" She responds seriously without hesitation: "You first need a mentor, a supervisor who will work closely with you (i.e. the new employee) for maybe the first year, and lead until you really understand what is expected." After a pause, she adds what might be a whole second point: "You know, a person might work next to you all year and never reveal much of what's going on." A hint of the need for open and regular communication. Katya's responses proved prophetic.

(2) Well-oriented (American) employer. Elsewhere, a Russian onsite manager of a joint enterprise turns our question away from the employ*ee* to the employ*er*. She responds that the American manager or onsite consultant—whoever will employ or supervise an educated Russian—needs a good orientation to the current business culture and the conditions for doing business in Pacific Russia. She reflects the fact that, too often, an American business expert brings knowledge based only on experience in the U.S. context, or perhaps other societies. "The tax system and commercial laws here just now—*not* the Russian personnel—pose the hardest problems for a new enterprise," she emphasizes. But she has more to say.

(3) Winning confidence. Taking the time and care to learn the local culture and business practices, she observes, will help an American employer to win the confidence of his Russian colleagues—whether partners or employees. This theme emerged in most interviews, beginning with the Russian manager cited here. It has several strands.

(a) Are you going to stay? Word is out that *some* Americans come to this new economic frontier with no intention of staying long. These are either schemers and con artists so familiar on America's own frontier, or traveling salesmen, or simply have no patience for a long-term investment. So the Russian partner or employee seeks reassurance as to the durability of the American partner or employer. "Will it be worth the trouble?"

(b) What chance of success? Economic conditions themselves are in such flux—and for most Russians, disarray—that by now an educated Pacific Russian will likely greet a new financial venture with skepticism or immense caution. "What reason have Russian youth to feel positive toward anything?" exclaims one who left a high academic position to help match Russian youth with new multinational ventures in this region. "Since 1989 (or longer) there's been no place for them in the economy, no one asks them to work." He means that, *even after* landing a good entry job, the young Russian employee needs special assurance that he/she can invest personal confidence in the deal. Again the question, "Is this really going to be a durable relationship?"

(c) **Do you respect us?** A third strand lies in the potential friction between cultures at one certain rubbing point. On the Russian side, others have long discussed the question of whether low self-esteem is a national characteristic. Whatever its roots, there is an anxiety today among young Russians, a self-doubt about their society-at-large sometimes concealed under an assertive *"Of course* I can do that" [tone implies "Do you think we're all so backward?"]. The American entrepreneur who takes seriously that sensitivity can avoid a lot of misunderstanding.

Further Response by Russian Senior Co-Workers.

The American salesman. A historical characteristic of Americans willing to venture into new territory is "salesman's bravado," an optimism sustained sometimes by whistling in the dark. [The fact that this is a cliche is, itself, revealing.] Sometimes this otherwise harmless habit shows up as joking or teasing of co-workers in response to their serious question. Now overlay this evasive joking onto someone on the team who harbors self-doubt. So, where these characteristics (Russian and American) meet one another, especially in an employer-employee relationship, they clash. One can see that great potential for unintended "put-downs" or just plain miscommunication. What feels to the American like light joking or mild correction could, for the Russian, lead to building up a psychological barricade to defend one's pride or self-esteem. This does not at all mean that the Russian lacks a sense of humor! That humor normally is robust. But a sound relationship could be sabotaged by this one category of conflict. So both sides must learn this.

(4) Informal bonding across cultures. A Russian instructor at a VUZ in the Far East with strong professional ties in Alaska observes (1996) that "within the past five years, the new young graduates from programs in economics and business management have significantly more self-assurance than their predecessors, and they seem to know more as well." Yet she, too, stresses the need for U.S. entrepreneurs to devote the effort needed for understanding this generation of Russians. "Maybe they should go to a *banya* with Russian acquaintances, and just sit and talk and listen sometimes," she says earnestly. The *banya* is not only a steam bath; it also is an occasion for a group of men—or of women—to relax with food and drink and stories and laughter. It is a uniquely Russian institution where much of the culture comes together. "There still are important psychological and cultural differences," our instructor warns.

(5) Working as team member. A professor of medicine, sophisticated in U.S.-Russian initiatives in the Russian Far East, keenly observes that highly educated Russian and North Americans have different ways of working together in groups. In the American working group, he observes, each member normally has a carefully defined role. Once given these role assignments, people tend to avoid meddling in one anothers' work as they "encapsulate" themselves with the help of technology and become self-reliant within their own space. (This Russian in fact used the term "capsular.")

In a typical Russian working group, on the other hand, the group itself *remains* the decision center, and each member remains more continuously attentive to the leader for initiative and direction.

This keen observation by the professor would imply, then, that the new Russian employee/colleague may need encouragement to take greater individual responsibility and initiative as a team member in the enterprise. Yet it implies, also, that an American supervisor needs to know about this cultural difference.

American Responses.

When the same question—i.e. about needs of graduates from Pacific Russia's VUZy—is put to North Americans on site, they agree with most of the foregoing comments. These American respondents have made Pacific Russia their second home for a year or more, and have actively engaged in screening Russian applicants for responsible positions there. Most of those whom they hired have become their own associates.

(1) Trust. One keen businessman had arrived relatively early in the era of *perestroika,* and developed an extensive marketing operation. By

1994–95 his staff consisted of eight to ten home-base employees, Russians and Americans, and the company prospered. But in 1996 he gave an emphatic, one-word reply to the question about what highly-trained young Russian employees still needed: "Trust!" he said with a poignant look. "They must learn to trust me, and to be trustworthy themselves." He did not delve into specific experiences that generated the heat behind this answer. He went on to elaborate, however.

This western American—call him "Dave"—has a direct and open manner, and a humanitarian's heart. He installed an experienced Russian accountant as second in command, a bright and clever Russian woman in charge of marketing, and several venturesome Americans in other staff positions. He himself remained probably the only one without much skill in Russian language. At the time of the interview, two misfortunes (one was Stateside) had combined to mount a serious threat to the firm's survival.

During this period, apparently, staff communication had begun to flow *around* Dave rather than *to* him and word of problems sometimes did not reach him on time for his corrective action. The interviewer noticed that at least two American staff members had left rather abruptly for the U.S. One of those, according to others, lacks a mature sense of personal responsibility. So it is not hard to surmise, in this case, that Dave's closest confidantes—not American but Russian colleagues—failed to clue him in about some impending problem brewing with the American "outside person." *This surmise remains speculative.* Yet it is still useful for illustration. In a communication sense David, though the on-site CEO, remained an outsider.

(2) Sense of Team. Pacific Russians tend to be more open, direct and spontaneous than their countrymen in European Russia. Yet, professional employees do not always bring this direct and open manner to the job. In the culture of an office, they see information as a valuable resource; so they may keep it until it can be traded for something they want. (Maybe more of a reflex than conscious intent.) The close teamwork of the student's group through university years does not transfer at once to a co-worker team in a new job. It is likely that "Dave," despite his natural generosity, had not yet won the "this-is-my-team" confidence of his Russian co-workers by the time some bad news should have been reported to him. At the same time, one should not assume that a Russian professional confides more readily in other *Russians* than in American colleagues. In fact, it can be just the opposite, especially if language is not a problem. Examples of this are not rare.

105

An aggressive American manager with good Russian language skills became field director in the Far East for a U.S.–funded project. He had more than two years of work experience in the RFE when he assumed this position. Our interview question drew from—call him Doug—a detailed discussion of his screening process for new staff and his subsequent satisfaction with their performance. Doug advertised and then personally interviewed more than twenty applicants, all with higher education. He claims to have quickly gained the trust of those he selected, to the level where they joined his competitive spirit and saw certain local Russians as problematic to their common effort. They would warn him of possible threats to their success. Like a pro hockey team with Russian, American, and Canadian players, they attained loyalty to their enterprise, beyond nationalities. It seems important to point out, however, that Doug had the ability to invite "his team" to a nearby hotel for coffee, tea or beer and informal conversation *in Russian*. Whatever Doug did to shape his team, he reports that in due time they began to take iniative to tell him how to gain advantage over their organization's competitors. They shared and accepted responsibility for the success of their common enterprise.

Indicators of Technical Readiness.

Most VUZy lack the quantity of current equipment now available to most American undergraduate students. University libraries still function with card catalogues, not the new electronic search systems in California libraries today. Periodical collections lag far behind those of U.S. academic libraries (which themselves complain of severe and growing budget limitations). An old university widely-known for its work in the humanities lacks a microfilm "reader" that can print hardcopy pages for the user. Even smooth chalkboards for classrooms remain in short supply. A dean in a large U.S. medical school tops his list of contrasts with the fact that a U.S. medical intern can call up onto his (computer) screen a list of symptoms or new pharmaceuticals to help him deal with a given client, and (the dean) assumes that his Russian counterpart has not experienced that.

This type of critique is mostly accurate, and has been for a long time. So how important is it with regard to the competency of those who graduate? Most U.S. corporations expect to orient new employees—American or otherwise—to the company's own specific equipment and techniques.

After orientation and practice with the technology involved in a particular workplace, the average Russian graduate should require no more assistance of this nature than any other graduate. For simple math tasks, however, one might find the *Russian* depending less on a calculator.

Depth vs. Breadth. Probably the most common observation, when comparing Russian with U.S. higher educational outcomes, holds that Russian undergraduates emerge with more thorough grounding in theoretical knowledge, U.S. undergraduates with more breadth and diversity of ideas. In mathematics and physics, U.S. professors generally concede that a Russian undergraduate has at least a year's advance over his average U.S. counterpart. For majors in philology and languages, one also can make a persuasive case. In certain of the arts it also is demonstrable. In history, however, and philosophy and social sciences before the 1990s scholars say a student had no choice at all: the theory was fixed and conclusions had to turn out to be Marxist-Leninist. Currently courses in the "new" economics and in business management have become growth industries within educational institutions. These show a heavy influence by British and American scholars.

So, at least in scientific and technical fields, Russian college graduates bring a thorough grounding in basic principles. They still have few electives, and practically none outside the major. In the liberal arts they have less breadth, although that is increasing now. After high school they study and train directly toward a profession or occupation, and thus generally advance further in their specialization in the first diploma program (usually five years) than do their North American counterparts.

In contrast, American students squeeze into their program many explorations beside their major, and many then change their major part way through. Traditionally the American college bachelor's degree is, by design, *pre*-professional—e.g. pre-medical, pre-law, pre-theological. Today's B.A. and B.S. programs are highly individuated, tailored to suit the individual student's aims. Whatever weaknesses this may have, it generally is conceded to increase the student's flexibility and adaptability in years beyond graduation.

Increasingly, administrators in American institutions market their programs to prospective students with promises to produce "job readiness" (employability, etc.); they try to avoid the very "non-essential" subjects which have made their own alumni more flexible, adaptable! So there is some convergence as both systems strive toward similar student outcomes.

Comparing Academic Programs. Earlier we compared features of the experience of being an undergraduate in universities of Pacific Russia and of California. With some overlap, the following discussion focusses on what students have gained as they emerge from the two respective systems.

Estimating "equivalency" between the educational products of one university and those of another never can become an exact science. Yet in practice it often becomes necessary to compare the graduates, the "outcomes" by examining curricular structure and other aspects of higher educational institutions, both domestically and between countries. So one can face the sweeping question, "How do graduates from higher education institutions (VUZy) in Pacific Russia compare with American counterparts?" by comparing what goes into their preparation. Admittedly that yields only one kind of comparison.

(a) **The prestige game.** Don't get into it! In Russia just as in the United States there is a pecking order among universities and institutes. Prestige of an institution, whether social or academic, indeed gives to its diploma extra influence in job-seeking and other social contacts. In Russia today (as in the former USSR), Moscow State University still gets the most respect and (in general) has the most renowned scholars on its teaching staff. State Universities in St. Petersburg and, interestingly, Novosibirsk, follow in that order (though varying by discipline). Americans of course have a parallel social placement list in the top members of the "Ivy League" plus Berkeley, Stanford and Chicago. Yet the *diplom spetsialista* (first university degree) in Russia still follows rather standard outlines for each field and major discipline, despite the individuation and regionalizing described in previous chapters. A national *"attestatsionaya kommissiya"* (comp.: accrediting commission) still gives to all VUZy a periodic (normally five-year) inspection and approval.

The *diplom spetsialista* remains the first university-level degree in Russia regardless of the prestige of the institution bestowing it. Similarly, a U.S. bachelor's degree is not called something else (e.g. "master's") if conferred by Harvard.

In some cases, a proud and excellent Russian university may provide an English translation of its own five-year *diplom*, and call it a "master's degree." This may be more of a statement of quality assurance, however, than an analytical comparison with the actual nature of the American master's degree in that field. It may miss significant differences in structure and aim of the comparable U.S. program, even if the Russian graduate does "know more" of the specialty in a quantitative sense. Equivalency questions involve more than (a) quantity of technical knowledge acquired and (b) reputation of the institution.

Thus in analyzing the comparability of graduates from Pacific Russia, one is well-advised to count a first university *diplom* in, say, chemistry or engineering or English, without regard to prestige-ranking of the particular institution that issued it. This corresponds to the common requirement of an (American) personnel office that a job applicant have "a bachelor's" degree in X f ield, without providing a list of preferred institutions. For this purpose, a bachelor of arts/science degree is a bachelor of arts/science degree, if it comes from an accredited institution. So in Russia, a *diplom spetsialista* is a *diplom spetsialista* regardless of which (recognized) institution it came from. Within a given discipline, scholars may weight where the "strongest" departments are, but even there the sands can shift.

(b) Time-span(s) for learning. Educated Russians frequently assume that, since they spent five years on their first university degree and presented a "thesis," they naturally have the equivalent in the U.S. of a master's degree. As seen above, their university may even inform them that this is the case. Determining actual equivalency, however, presents much more complexity than total timespans. Consider the following elements of that complexity.

—Ten or eleven years vs. twelve in elementary/secondary school.

—The American "four years to the bachelor's degree" itself has become hypothetical. For various reasons, most undergraduates in U.S. colleges and universities today take five or more years to graduate. Some majors have been structured as five-year programs; others are just too tough to work through in the ideal time; and many American students change their major in midstream, thus broadening but stretching the time needed for their completion. And this only refers to *full-time* students, who are no longer the norm.

—In many cases, the Russian undergraduate program, with a specialization (major) and perhaps a substantial minor, includes all courses in education, pedagogy, and practice teaching required for teaching the student's major subject. In most American states these represent another year *after* the baccalaureate major and degree.

—In practice, the length of a Russian semester (historically) has varied, at least because of the use of students for bringing in the harvest. For first year and some second year students in Pacific Russia this practice continues well into the 1990s. Russian agriculture makes far less use than

109

the U.S. does of importing cheap "guest worker" farm labor. For first and second year students, actual instruction therefore may not have begun until November instead of 1 September. (Of course, not all populated areas have tillable land.)

—The lecture or instructional hour in Russia is defined as forty-five minutes rather than U.S. convention of fifty minutes. Most Russian classes occur as "a pair," two academic hours back-to-back for eighty-five to ninety minutes (maximum), but the basic definition holds. This is a 10 percent difference.

—The *uchebniy plan* (detailed outline of a specific degree/specialization program) distinguishes the number of hours to be spent in lectures, in lab/seminars, and in practice. But the list of courses and final grades usually provided with the diploma shows at most the total hours involved in each course, with no breakdown by type. So simply seeing these figures (total hours) does not offer a sufficient guide for calculating "semester credit units" earned in a particular subject. *By itself,* the "total hours" figure cannot even serve as a proxy measure of the level of learning attained.

—The Russian "diploma thesis" is, of course, analogous to the American "Senior paper" or "graduation project" that caps many bachelor's degree programs. The "year's project" (*kursovaya rabota*) that accompanies some courses, though shown separately on the transcript, is analogous to the American term paper.

Thus, the amount of time spent on the Russian first VUZ-level degree—even for full-time students—most resembles that spent on a U.S. bachelor's degree, including one to two semesters often used for teacher preparation courses and practice teaching.

Content. It would be a serious mistake, however, to *under*estimate the product of current-day Russian higher education. Despite many recent curricular changes and experiments in VUZy of Pacific Russia, one generalization still holds firm: students tend to progress further *in their major* than do their American counterparts. The five-year program concentrates on the chosen specialization, aims straightway for the professional job envisioned (and, often, for teaching it). Some other subjects are required in the first two years—history, philosophy, now substantially freed from former ideological blinders, and foreign language are standard although the hours vary. Yet, for better or worse, the Russian undergraduate cannot explore and wander in a forest of elective (breadth) courses as can the typical American student. The student is focused on the fixed major theme. This complicates the task of comparison.

110

American mathematicians, as well as scholars in physics, generally have found that, between Russian and U.S. undergraduates of similar years, the Russian typically has advanced further in those disciplines (math. and physics). The same may be true for other basic science disciplines. Engineering varies by field. Those fields involving outdoor construction, for example, may lack training with new lighter weight materials, due partly to conservatism about what the region's climatic conditions would tolerate. Computer engineering, on the other hand, benefits from its relatively recent introduction to undergraduates in the civilian sphere, Japanese interests in cultivating new relations with the Russian Far East, and enrollment growth in this specialization in the 1990s. Here, firm grounding in theory and basics (and in English communication) has been more important than knowledge of this week's newest release by X computer firm. Information and communication have long been of special interest in this extremity of the Russian Federation. Aerospace design engineers, in some U.S. expert opinions, rate among the best in those interrelated fields.

For different reasons, Russian specialists in Russian philology and language teaching seem able to advance faster in those disciplines than their U.S. counterparts. Native speakers of Russian, they are immersed in Slavic verbal culture and literature from birth. The reverse is true of majoring in English language and literature. Most English/American literature is read in Russian translation, many advanced classes are conducted in Russian. But English grammatical rules and terminology, especially those pertaining to verb forms, are memorized in fine detail by the Russian student majoring in English language. In that sense the Russian student typically may receive a more thorough *analytical* grounding even in English.

This is not to say, as some Americans tend to repeat, that "they are just naturally better at languages than we are." Those who major in English language and prepare to teach it generally attain a good level of competence in using and teaching it. One should not assume, however, that this naturally prepares them as interpreters. Some interpreters do attain high levels of proficiency. But endless American idioms provide much room for misunderstanding.

Corporate lessons learned. The international business manager of a large U.S. company recently reflected on experiences of his firm in establishing an office in the Russian Far East. Pertinent to working relationships with Russian business colleagues, he offered the following suggestions.

1. Understand the partner's motivations and intentions, as he must understand yours, for entering partnership. Plan to stay involved for the long-term, and make this clear to the Russian partner. An expectation of quick and easy profit can bring down the whole effort.
2. Commit to an on-site presence.
3. One cannot take for granted clear, ongoing communication. Must work at this continuously.
4. In selection and training of local employees, attitudes prove even more important than professional skills. Does the prospective local employee show signs of being not only willing but eager to learn? Also, attitudes of patience and persistence can be learned, therefore can be taught (inculcated).
5. Take time and care to celebrate step-by-step successes.
6. Stay in close touch with on-site team. (Implies more than flying site director back to corporate HQ periodically.)

(10/31/97 presentation in San Francisco, by Beatt Ammann, Bus. Mgr. CIS Operations, Caterpillar Co.; rep. in RFE by Amur Machinery & Svc.)

These points of succinct advice from Mr. B. Ammann, directed to American businesspeople, correspond closely to the foregoing summary of what the local (Pacific Russian) employee/co-worker might need most for a successful working relationship with Americans in Pacific Russia. Through a normal screening process, *the needed professional skills and capabilities can be found.* It is, rather, cultural and attitudinal factors that play the pivotal roles in building successful teamwork.

He/she needs: (a) to understand your (the American employer/partner's) actual aims and intentions; (b) to have your actual presence frequently; (c) to communicate (i.e. give-and-take) regularly, clearly; (d) to learn that, in a market economic culture, dogged persistence and patient courtesy are key virtues; (e) to share positive feed-back and active acknowledgment of successful efforts, including team efforts.

Generational culture. A story about generational cultures may prove useful at this point. An American world traveler and cosmopolitan person hosted a Russian exchange student from Khabarovsk in his California home for a monthlong holiday from the university. Both host and guest spoke the other's language well. When the guest student asked about a particular style of American vehicle, however, his host did not recognize the terminology, and tried to correct the guest. Eventually, however, the (older) host found that his Russian guest had used an accurate term for an American-made vehicle which he (the host) never heard before. Later, the young Russian inquired about a current American musician widely known in Pacific Russia but unknown to the host in California. These, of course, illustrate cultural differences *between generations,* not between different nations. Young people of Pacific Russia and Pacific America share together some knowledge which their elders commonly do not share.

Conclusion

Students in Pacific Russia, a place which a decade ago seemed remote and strange to American businesspeople, resemble young American students more than they differ from them. Although they've grown up in Asia, their roots are mostly European, with a new twist. Their grandparents or parents, a majority of them reared in traditional European ways, had adapted to practical requirements of life in frontier towns and cities. Then they clustered increasingly in cities and increasingly attended higher educational institutions. Students in Pacific Russia today are overwhelmingly urban, not "frontiersmen." Now for a decade, while still invisible to most foreign eyes, they have been moving to the musical beat of their generation worldwide. They are tuned in to their generation, and to their peers in North America today—more than the other way around. They are preparing for meaningful professional roles in the emerging interaction around the Pacific Rim. They are the "readiest resource" of Pacific Russia and, if hard times require it, also the most mobile.

Appendix A

60+ Higher Educational Institutions (VUZy) in Pacific Russia 1996[1]

City and Institute:	Full-time	Other	Total
Angarsk			
Angarsk Technological Institute	1,582	763	2,345
Birobidzhan			
Birobidzhan State Pedagogical Institute	760	190	950
Blagoveshchensk			
Blagoveshchensk State Medical Institute			2,400
Blagoveshchensk Polytechnical Institute	1,800	700	2,500
Far East State Agrarian University	3,946	1,000	4,946
Bratsk			
Bratsk Industrial Institute	3,000	2,000	5,000
Buryat (See Ulan Ude)			
Chita			
Chita State Medical Institute			
Chita State Pedagogical Institute	3,600	1,600	5,200
Chita Polytechnical Institute			
East Siberia (See Ulan Ude)			
Far Eastern (See Khabarovsk and Vladivostok)			
Irkutsk			
Irkutsk State University	4,300	4,400	8,700
Irkutsk State Economics Academy	3,200	1,997	5,107
Irkutsk State Pedagogical Institute	3,300	2,800	6,100
Irkutsk State Inst. Of Foreign Language Teaching			3,000
Irkutsk State Medical Institute			
Irkutsk State Polytechnical Institute	5,000		5,000
Irkutsk Institute of Rail Transport Engineering	1,500	3,500	5,000
Irkutsk Agricultural Institute			4,500
Russo-Asian Liberal Arts University (branch of private VUZ in Ekaterinburg)			350
Khabarovsk			
Khabarovsk State Technical University	4,729	2,127	6,856
Khabarovsk State Pedagogical University	3,500	1,500	5,000
Khabarovsk State Medical University	3,200	650	3,860
Khabarovsk State Institute of Arts & Culture			1,522

115

60+ Higher Educational Institutions (VUZy) in Pacific Russia 1996[1]

City and Institute:	Enrollment[2]		
	Full-time	Other	Total
Khabarovsk State Institute of Physical Culture	600	600	1,200
Khabarovsk State Institute of Pharmacy			
Khabarovsk State Academy of Economics & Law	2,354	1,817	4,171
Khabarovsk Military Institute for Federal Border Patrol	N/A	N/A	N/A
Far East State Academy of Communication Ways (Rail Transport)	4,058	3,637	7,695
Far East Institute of Management & Business	127	455	582
Far East Academy of Public Admin. (Service)	668	714	1,382
*Far Eastern College, Moscow Univ. of Consumer Cooperatives	223	100	323
Siberian State Academy of Telecommunications & Informatics (External Fac.)			
Far East Institute of Legislative & Legal Studies			
Far East Institute of Agronomics & Business			
*Pacific Institute of Economics & Law			
St. Petersburg Inst. of Foreign Economic Relations, Economics and Law (Branch)			
Komsomol'sk-na-Amure			
Komsomol'sk n.A. Pedagog. Institute	2,100	1,400	2,500
Komsomol'sk n.A. Polytechnical Institute	2,700	950	3,650
Magadan			
International Pedagogical University	1,500	688	2,188
Petropavlovsk-Kamchatskii			
Kamchatka State Pedagogical Institute	1,000	500	1,500
Petropavlovsk-Kamch. Maritime Engineering College			
Kamchatka Institute of International Business			
Ulan Ude			
Buryat State University (includes Buryat Ped. Institute)	4,000	1,800	5,800
Buryat Agricultural Institute	2,400	2,200	4,600
East Siberia Technological Institute	4,000	2,400	6,400
East Siberia State Institute of Culture	1,000	2,000	3,000
Ussuriisk			
Ussuriisk State Pedagogical Institute	3,000	1,400	4,400
Primorskii Agricultural Institute			2,800
Vladivostok			
Far East State University	4,500	3,000	7,500
Vladivostok Medical Institute			
Far East State Maritime Academy	1,900	1,500	3,400

60+ Higher Educational Institutions (VUZy) in Pacific Russia 1996[1]

City and Institute:	Enrollment[2]		
	Full-time	Other	Total
Far East State Technical University			
Far East State Institute of Arts			
Far East Commercial Institute	2,300	2,300	4,600
Far East Technical Institute of Fish Industry & Economics			
Far East Institute of Consumer Services			
Regional Educational Center for International Cooperation			
Yakutsk			
Yakutsk State University	6,639	3,031	9,670
Yakutsk Agricultural Institute			
Yuzhno-Sakhalinsk			
Yuzhno-Sakhalinsk State Pedagogical Institute			
Yuzhno-Sakhalinsk Technical-Economics College			
*Sam Yuk Institute			
Subtotals:	88,486	[3]	155,637

Estimating from a sample, from 10% to 18% of these numbers graduate each year.

1. List is not presented as exhaustive. In particular, the Maritime Territory (*Primorskii krai*) probably has more independent VUZy than shown. Office in Vladivostok did not respond to inquiries. This table is estimated as accounting for 90 percent of enrollment in 1997. "Pacific Russia" defined as extending from Irkutsk Oblast' eastward to the Pacific, does not include some portions of Eastern Siberia.
2. When not available from firsthand sources, enrollment data in Appendix A derive from the catalog-directory, *Vysshie uchebyne zavedeniya rossiiskoi federatsii* (Higher Educational Institutions of the Russian Federation), Udmurt Univ. Press, Izhevsk, 1994. All data fall within years 1993–1996.
3. Because of the varying numbers of institutions reporting, this tally would make quoting of it too deceptive. The day full-time student tally already is an underestimate, and is closer to 100,000 with all institutions accounted for.

117

Appendix B

Glossary, Selected Terminology of Russian Higher Education with Nearest American Equivalents

arkhivnaya spravka	academic transcript, incl. hours and grades, as kept by registrar.
aspirant(ka)	graduate student. (fem.)
aspirantura	graduate study.
assistent	graduate assistant or lecturer. (Not "assistant professor.")
attestat	certificate of high school completion (h.s. diploma).
diplomnaya rabota	graduation paper or project; "senior paper."
doktorskaya stepen'	doctoral degree, the scholarly degree after *Kandidat nauk,* conferred after major book publication and wide recognition by peers in the same field.
dotsent	academic teaching rank attainable approx. 5 years after *Kand. nauk* is received; equiv. to "Associate Professor" except it is portable among institutions.
ekzamen	final exam. for a course, usually consisting of 3 questions drawn by lot, answered orally before a panel of instructors.
fakul'tet	school, college or division within an institution of higher education; e.g. School of Pediatric Medicine, College of Engineering
gumanitarnye	liberal arts (humanities + social sciences + misc.)
kafedra	"chair," acad. department led by a senior scholar.

kandidat nauk	first scholarly degree (beyond magister if any), earned by 3-year directed study, qualifying examinations, then a time period for dissertation and defense.
kolichestvo studentov	total enrollment, number enrolled.
kollektiv	student body of an institution.
kontrol'naya rabota	written test or quiz.
kurs	(a) numbered year/level in undergraduate study. (b) course, often not semester-length.
kursovaya rabota	term paper; grade is recorded separately from course grade on transcript.
nauchnyi	(adj.) (a) scientific; (b)scholarly; (c) systematic.
NII—nauchnyi issledovat el'skii institut	Scientific Research Inst., under Academy of Sciences.
para	A "pair" of instructional hours @ 45 min. "back-to-back" for a classroom period of up to 90 minutes.
pismennyi	written
prepodavatel'	instructor; i.e. any member of instructional staff, any rank.
professor	"full" professor (*only*)
pyatyorka	a grade of "5" (excellent) in Russian grading system.
sostav' (professorskii prepodavatel'skii)	in U.S. terms, the whole faculty.
student—(contrast *shkolnik*)	one who studies for the first university-level degree in a higher educational institution; (contrast "school pupil.")
svidetel'stvo	certificate
uchebnyi	instructional; having to do with teaching-learning matters.
uchebnyi plan	detailed curriculum for one major or specialization.
uchyonnyi	scholar; scholarly
vypiska (iz zachyotnoi vedomosti	official list of subjects and final grades, document comes with specialist's diploma and matching serial number.
vypusknik	recent graduate (alumnus/a) of university or other VUZ.
vypustit'	to graduate (vb.)

vysshaya shkola	higher education, usually in sense of the sector or industry, as Americans use the term "academia."
vysshee obrazovanie	higher education—process and successful result.
vysshee uchebnoe zavedenie (v.u.z.)	institution of higher education.
zachyot	grade notation meaning "pass" or "may continue."
zachyotnaya knizhka	booklet with sequential record of courses, grades, and instructor sign-offs carried by student (shows each semester).

Bibliography

Azulay & Azulay. *The Russian Far East.* New York, Hippocrene Books, 1995.

Bobrick, Benson. *East of the Sun—Epic conquest and tragic history of Siberia.* New York: Henry Holt & Co., N.Y., 1992.

Burdukovskaya, V.G. *Istoriya narodnogo obrazovaniya vostochnoi sibiri* (History of Public Education in Eastern Siberia.) Irkutsk, Russia, Irkutsk State Pedagogical Institute, 1994.

Dal'nii Vostok Rossii—ekonomika investitsii kon'iunktura; Jan. 1977. (Russian Far East: Economics, Investment, State of the Market); Information quarterly by the Russian-American Far Eastern Center for Economic Development, Vladivostok [Tel./Fax (4232) 26-67-74].

DeSouza, P. *Territorial Production Complexes in the Soviet Union—with special focus on Siberia;* Univ. of Gothenburg, Sweden; 1989. (Cf. esp. section 5.4.2, "The Nature of the Manpower Problem," pp. 198–206.)

Drysdale, P. & M. O'Hare, eds. *The Soviets and the Pacific Challenge.* Armonk, N.Y.: M.E. Sharpe, Inc. 1991. Foreword by E.A. Shevardnadze. Papers from an international scholarly conference, Feb. 1990.

California Postsecondary Education Commission: *Education Needs of California Firms for Trade in Pacific Rim Markets.* Staff report to the Commission; Sacramento, Calif.: Dec. 1988. (Dale M. Heckman was principal staff and author.)

California Postsecondary Education Commission: *Looking to California's Pacific Neighborhood—Roles for Higher Education.* Sacramento, 1987. (Dale M. Heckman, principal staff and author.)

Center for Strategic and International Studies, "The Russian Economy in October 1997"; Washington, D.C.; report 27 Oct. 1997. (Keith Bush, Dir., Russian and Eurasian Program.)

Gos. Kom. Rossiiskoi Federatsii po vysshemy obrazovaniu: *Gosudarstvennyi obrazovatel'nyi standart vysshego professional'nogo obrzaovaniya (izdanie ofitsial'noe);* Moscow; 1995. (Federal academic standards for professional higher education.)

Gos. kom. SSSR po statistike: *Naselenie SSSR 1987;* Statisticheskii sbornik; Moscow, 1988. *Chislennost' naseleniya RSFSR po dannym vsesoiuznoi perepisi naseleniya 1989 goda;* Moscow, 1990. (Popul'n. statistics of Russian Federation, Census of 1989)

Heckman, D., "Changing Higher Education in Siberia," in D. Whittaker, ed.; *International Relations, National Policies, and Higher Education in the Pacific Region;* Faculty of Education, Univ. of British Columbia, Vancouver, 1990.

————"Studying East Russia," in *NewsNet,* the newsletter of the AAASS (American Assoc. for Advancement of Slavic Studies), Oct. 1993. One-page argument for the conceptual unity or coherence of the region from Irkutsk Oblast' to the Pacific edge of Russia.

Kinelev, V.G. *Ob'ektivnaya neobkhdimost—Istoria, problemy i perspekitivy reformirovaniya vysshego obrazovaniya Rossi;* Respublika Publishers, Moscow, 1995. ("An Objectiv Necessity—History, Problems & Perspectives on Reforming Higher Education in Russia") Kinelev was Minister of Higher Education, Russian Federation.

Kotkin, S. and D. Wolff, ed. *Rediscovering Russia in Asia—Siberia and the Russian Far East;* Armonk, N.Y., M.E. sharpe Inc., 1995.

Organization for Economic Cooperation & Development (OECD): *Labour Market Dynamics in the Russian Federation (Proceedings);* Centre for Cooperation with Economies in Transition, Paris, 1997. (Papers from a workshop in Moscow, December 1996).

Osnovnye napravleniye perestroiki vysshego i srednego obrazovaniya v strane, Moscow, 1987. (Official statement of new federal polices for higher and secondary education)

Russian Far East News; Alask Ctr. For Internat'l. Business, Univ. of Alaska–Anchorage; a monthly newsletter. Discontinued by grant budget in July 1997.

Russian Far East Update; "a monthly business briefing"; Seattle, Washington.

Savel'iev., A. Ya: *Prepodavateli v vysshikh uchebnykh zavedeniyakh SSSR (kratkaya spravka)* "The Teaching Faculty in Higher Educational Institutions of the USSR—a short inquiry"); Federeal Research Institute on Higher Education, Moscow; June 1991. (Data from 1989; author was director of this research institute.)

Shakherova, Ol'ga, Prof., Letter concerning preparation of new courses, "Culture and Literature of Siberia" (incl. Indigenous languages). Irkutsk, 1995. (Unpublished.)

Smirnov, B.V., *"Gumanitarnoe obrazovanie v Khabarovskom gosudarstvennom tekhnicheskom universitete"* (Liberal arts education in Khabarovsk State Technical University), Khabarovsk, 1993. An internal working paper, 4 pp. Prof. Smirnov is the founding dean of KhSTU's School of Liberal Arts.

Spravochnik dlya postupaiuschchikh v vysshie uchebnye zavedeniya SSSRa, Moscow; annual official publication, "Directory for Those Entering Higher Educational Institutions of the USSR."

124

Sravnidannye pokazateli sotsial'-no-ekonomicheskogo polozheniya regionov Rossiiskoi Federatsii; T.I.M., 1995. ("Comparative indicators of the socio-economic situation of the regions of the Russian Federation"; these data were provided from computer files at the Far East Economics Research Institute, Khabarovsk, courtesy of Motrych, E.)

Stephan, John & V.P. Chichkanov, eds. *Soviet-American Horizons on the Pacific.* Univ. of Hawaii Press, 1986.

Stephan, J.J., "The Russian Far East," in *Current History,* Oct. 1993 (pp. 331–336).

———. *The Russian Far East—A History;* Stanford Univ. Press, 1994.

SUPAR Report: a semiannual compilation of news items mostly from the press in various cities of the Northern Pacific region; Ctr. For Russia-in-Asia, Univ. of Hawaii, Honolulu. Discontinued by grant budget.

Swearingen, R. (ed.): *Siberia and the Soviet Far East.* Hoover Institution Press, 1987. (Cf. esp. chapter by V. Connolly, "Siberia Yesterday, Today, and Tomorrow," section on "Population and labor.")

Wood, Alan & R.A. French, eds. *The Development of Siberia—People and Resources.* New York: St. Martin's Press, 1989. (Papers from conference of April 1986.) Cf. esp. T.I.Zaslavskaya et al, "Social Development of Siberia: Problems, Possible Solutions" (Chapt. 8).

Yelyutin, V.P.: *Higher Education in a Country of Developed Socialism;* Vysshaya Shkola Publishers, Moscow; 1980. English transl. (700 pp.) in issues of *Soviet Education, a journal of translations,* July 1984–Oct. 1985. Review by D.M. Heckman in *Comparative Education Review,* Fall 1987.